Secrets In The Tides
A Family Saga

Roberta M. O'Connell

Mary Bayne Wojdylak

Princess Publishers
P.O. Box 178
North Uxbridge, MA 01538

Photos Used by Permission of:
Roberta M. O'Connell &
Mary Bayne Wojdylak

Dedicated to those we love and love us back. Thank you, Jesus for the gift of family.

A special dedication to my husband, Dave who is the love of my life; and to Jesus, who has given me the gift of a full life.
Roberta

This is dedicated to my wonderful husband, Jim of 48 years, my beautiful children and grandchildren and to my Lord and Savior Jesus Christ. All things are possible with God.
Mary

CHAPTER 1
THE HOMECOMING

I stood on the deck of the Islander; wind blowing through my hair and thoughts racing through my crowded mind. Although I had taken this journey many times in my life, this time was very different.

The closer the ferry got to the Island, the more restrictive my breathing became. I felt suffocated as panic took over; that kind of panic that makes you sweat and feel sick to your stomach; that kind of panic that makes the room spin and makes you want to scream at the top of your lungs, "HELP!!! I can't breathe!!" I felt trapped and I just wanted to jump over the side of the ship and swim back home to safety; to denial; to alcohol, which dulled the pain.

Three years ago I set out to lose myself in the city. Boston was a place where no one knew me and there would be no questions. I couldn't take the pity any longer.

You see, I had a twin brother named Shon and we were inseparable. In fact for a while I believed my name was Shonsharon because we were always spoken of as one. No one ever said; "Sharon, come here!" or "Shon, stop that!" If one was in trouble, it was assumed that both of us were involved.

Shon drowned in waters he knew better than anyone on the whole island of Martha's Vineyard. It was clouding up a bit when he set out on his own to pull up a couple of small nets and lobster traps he had dropped. It was really a two man job, but he didn't want to wait around with a storm on the horizon. I wasn't worried because my brother could smell bad weather. The air and the sea were a part of him and if he said he had time to do the job before the wind picked up, then I believed him.

Shon hadn't been feeling well the last couple of days before he died, so I think his internal barometer was off. Once he got out to the traps, the wind started gently blowing as the sky darkened. He didn't like stopping a job before it was finished, so he continued on to the nets. As he bent over the side of the small boat to grab the first net, a gust of wind knocked him right into the ocean.

That gale force wind came seemingly out of nowhere, capsizing the Boston Whaler, throwing Shon from the scene. He was a strong swimmer, but could not resurface. The trap ropes had become entangled around his ankle, dragging him to the bottom of the churning sea. He pulled with all his might against the weight of the full traps to no avail. The body of my sweet, handsome brother, Shon David Walsh would not be discovered for five long months.

I was told by the Harbor Patrol that his body was found tangled in the net. As strong a swimmer as he was, Shon was no match for the net that had entangled so many fish for him in the past.

My brother died on August 17, 2000; four days before our 21st birthday. We were to be 21 on the 21st; a once in a lifetime occurrence. We were planning a huge celebration with an old fashioned clam and lobster bake.

There's a great spot on South Beach where we love to go on a hot summer night, with a bunch of friends and dig a huge pit in the sand. That's where we begin to build our fire over rocks to make them really hot. Then we add the seaweed, lobsters, clams, corn on the cob from Mom's garden, linguica, kielbasa and potatoes! My mouth is watering just thinking about it. But this celebration was not to be. Not now. Not ever.

CHAPTER 2

Origins

Leaving Martha's Vineyard the day I buried my twin brother, I tried to lose myself in the city of Boston. I had an unlisted phone number and told no one from my past where I lived. Contact would keep the pain too close and make it all real; but somehow, they found me.

Unable to cope, I began to purge my thoughts onto page after page of crisp, white paper. Another year would pass before I would be done with this exercise in futility. Writing everything down only made me relive what I just could not face.

I was named for my great-great grandmother, Sharon Rose Walsh who hailed from Cork, Ireland. Mom used to tell me that I was one of those natural beauties, with long, flowing auburn hair and startling emerald eyes. All I saw was a face full of freckles, which Maggie always told me were a sign of beauty. When men looked at me I felt as though they were mocking me, but Dad would tell me it was because I was so beautiful. I still don't see it.

Being home again, I remember a time when my brother, Shon and I would play along the shallows of South Beach. We were about five years old when Shon yelled out, "Catch the fishy! Catch the fishy!" The man holding the net noticed just at that precise moment that Dad had snatched us twins out of the water, one under each arm and ran to the safety of the sandy beach. The "fishy" that Shon wanted to catch, turned out to be a large sand shark. Growing up on the ocean, we had no fear of the water or its inhabitants.

We were in a world all our own back then and were inseparable. It would be just about sixteen years later that tragedy would strike the Walsh family.

Long after the search had been given up, a boat full of partiers dropped anchor in the depths outside of the harbor so they could tan for a couple of hours. It took four of them to pull up the anchor thinking they were caught up on some seaweed. That day we got a visit from the Sheriff telling us that Shon's body had been found.

I remember receiving the news as if it was yesterday. Mom and I had just pulled into the driveway as the police cruiser arrived. It was surreal as the officer expelled the horrific details of my brother's death. I felt so helpless, so horrified, so guilty.

He was barely audible as my mind went in and out of consciousness. All I heard were these few words.

"...found.....body.....it's over....sorry.....so very sorry."

That's the moment when everything went black.

Some years would pass before the phone call. The voice on the other end was familiar as it repeated, "Sharon, dear, did ya hear me? Yer Mum and Da have gone to rest."

My parents, I was being told were both dead. They had a private plane and my dad piloted it. They were the only two on board when the plane crashed into the sea between Martha's Vineyard and Nantucket.

The nightmare I had so desperately tried to push deep into the past had suddenly become that thing that I could no longer ignore.

CHAPTER 3

Facing the Past

I'm 28 now, time to face my past; time to grow up. I'm all that's left of this family. Sitting in my car on this ferry, I feel so small and alone as the enormous doors open and we draw nearer to the dock. All at once I'm herded through those doors with no escape, ushered to the street. I was feeling claustrophobic surrounded by all the traffic and people racing around the cars.

I drove past the beach and my favorite ice cream shop, all places that I had been with my family. It reminded me of happier times when we were all together. The salt air and warm gentle breeze is relaxing as it flows freely through my convertible. At the same time I can't help feeling so bad that I abandoned my parents after such a loss. I've been gone way too long. Seven years is way too long, and now I'm too late.

CHAPTER 4

Maggie

As I turn the corner into my driveway, I see just past the willow tree, the voice I heard on the phone, running toward me, with her faithful old dog, Brandy in tow. How I've missed her face. She was always the one I went to when I was sad or needed to figure something out, like boys.

What a joy to see her still wearing the apron that I made for her in Home Economics. The apron ties flew behind her as her gray-streaked hair, braided down the middle of her back beat out a greeting. I always knew that there would be freshly baked Irish bread with golden raisins when I came home from school; no one cooked like my Maggie. I can almost taste her stew.

"Is that me Sharon, or is the sun playing tricks on me old eyes,"

Maggie cried? "It seems a lifetime since you've been ta home."

I jumped out of my car and ran to her like I did when I was scared of the thunderstorms. "It has been too long, Maggie. I've missed you so much."

Just then Maggie's dog, Brandy came running toward me, she was getting old, but still had a lot of puppy in her. She practically jumped into my arms as I bent down to hug her. "What is she Maggie, about 125?"

"She's just a puppy, she is," said Maggie. "And may I remind you that if it wasn't for Brandy you would have drowned when your beach chair folded up on you and you ended up head first in the ocean? It was Brandy, it was that came and got me to rescue your sorry self from the sea! And another thing..."

"I know, I know. I'm just teasing you Maggie; you're so easy to play with." When Maggie got going it was sometimes quite difficult to sort through her thick Irish brogue and it was also quite funny to listen to. This time when I hugged Maggie I didn't want to let her go.

We sat and talked over old times while we had the most delicious food prepared with love by Maggie of course. Never have I ever had its equal and I never want to leave this place again. I put some of Maggie's homemade beach plum jam on my scone and took a big sip of the Earl Grey tea that was just brewed in my grandmother's teapot, which she brought with her when she came to America as a young woman.

"The cottage never changes; it's always been a retreat for me. Thank you so much for warming the sitting room with the fire. It's so cozy and dinner was absolutely miraculous! I appreciate all the work you did here to get the cottage ready for me, Mags. I don't know what my family and I would have done without you all these years. There's no one like you. No one." I felt the loss of my family in that moment, wanting them here now, in this place, together again. I hung my head and barely in a whisper said, "I never should have left."

Trying to lighten the mood, as Maggie was so good at doing she said, "Oh, don't be silly Sharon, me darling. Brandy and me were so happy that you were coming home, don't you know, that it was just a labor of love, it was. I enjoy doing things for you."

"I'm sorry about disappearing Maggie. After Shon went missing, I ran and ran. I've put my life into my work until now. I've come back to chase away the ghosts that have been haunting me. Please help me

Maggie, I can't do this alone."
Maggie poured another cup of tea
for both of them to enjoy and
handed me the honey pot.

"I've taken to raising me own bees,
don't ya know! That there is from
right outside that door," Maggie said
as she pointed out the side entrance
to the gardens. Then she got up
and came over to me, brushing away
a tear on my cheek and whispered,
"you're Maggie's here, darlin'. I'm
not going anywhere. We'll get
through this together. I love you so
much, my sweet, sweet baby girl."

CHAPTER 5

Breakfast

"What an incredible morning!" I shouted to no one as I sprang from my bed. "The sun is shining, the seagulls are calling and the ocean is gently rolling onto the beach. I can't wait to look around. It's a new day." I always loved my room the best because it overlooked the ocean from the second floor. The sun came in every morning to wake me as I heard the song of the gulls floating by my window.

Sliding down the banister of the mahogany staircase, I was reminiscent of childhood days. As I strolled happily through the foyer, into the living room, past the dining room and into the kitchen, I was suddenly swept away by the aroma of freshly baked bread wafting through the air. I could practically taste the thick cut bacon and eggs fried in butter, which I'm sure Maggie will claim she churned just this morning, and my mouth salivated in anticipation of the buttermilk pancakes! Oh, happy day!

"Good morning, Maggie!" Then, looking at all the delicious food that Maggie had prepared, I proclaimed, "Good Lord, Maggie! If I eat like this all summer, I'll be fat and surely sink to the bottom of the ocean. Not to mention not being able to fit into all the new clothes I bought for this trip home." I suddenly felt a twinge of elation in the pit of my stomach and couldn't help but giggle. Home did that to me.

"Oh, go on with ya, child; ya look like ya could use a good meal, ya do. A wee little bird looks healthier than you." Maggie pinched my waist, but couldn't get a good grab. I was quite thin from anxiety.

"You're nothing but a bunch of skin and bones. Now sit down and eat up! I've made all y'er favorite dishes, including my homemade strawberry preserves. I just was putting them up before ya came. Thomas picked me a bushel of the biggest, juiciest strawberries I've seen from our patch in many a year, thanks to the good Lord for all the rain this year."

Maggie always felt such joy when people ate her food. She watched me eat every bite and beamed with pride as she cleaned up around me. "I forgot to tell ya that the good Dr. Michael Brennan came by jest t'other day to check up on the likes of me. He asked for ya, lass. Of course I went and told him all about y'er letter saying ya were coming home soon and don't ya know, Sharon dear, think I saw a twinkle in his eyes." Then, mischievously, she delivered this information; "I hear he's still single."

"Come on now Maggie. Every time I talk to you it's the same thing. Dr. Michael Brennan this and Dr. Michael Brennan that. I wasn't interested in him in High School and I'm not interested in him now. Mags, let's not argue; it's too beautiful a day. Can we please stop talking about Dr. What's-His-Name? Besides, I came here to see you, not pick up men."

"But...." Maggie tried.

"But nothing; now you promised! What do you say to a little boat ride in the Boston Whaler?" I scurried around the kitchen throwing random items into a picnic basket, then pulled Maggie out of the house and into the glorious sunshine.

"The dishes!" Maggie cried to no avail.

CHAPTER 6

Picnic in Paradise

On my lame attempt to help Maggie into the boat, she called back to me, "Oh, just wait 'til Thomas gets a load of you. He's getting along in years now, don't you know. That doesn't seem to stop him tending the gardens here though. He says it would a be a shame to let them go wild. Tell you the truth Sharon, I think it's what keeps him going. He's usually around here by the docks this time of morning after his fishing trip."

Slyly turning the tables on Maggie and her matchmaking I decided to be bold. "Are you two married yet? Thomas has been asking you for years and you still haven't said 'yes', I'm guessing. He's such a great guy and it's obvious that he loves you." I softened my tone yet still stirred a hornet's nest. I couldn't help but laugh at her reaction.

She was literally standing in the boat as it rocked wildly to her response. "I'm too old to be getting myself into marriage with the likes o' that man! Besides, when are you going to be marrying Dr. Brennan and bringing some life into this ole place," Maggie added in total sarcasm which was so funny coming from her.

Approaching the dock was Thomas, just in the nick of time. He was looking a bit older and more worn, but full of energy just the same as he carried his haul toward us.

"Thomas," I shouted in my excitement to see my dear, old friend! "Thomas!" I ran to him just as I always had as a child.

Thomas looked up and beamed. I could see youth in his beautiful blue eyes. Putting the basket of fish down, he picked up his pace and opened his arms to me. His hug was so comforting. It always was.

"Me and Maggie are going out for a ride; wanna come?"

"Not this time, Rosie." I had almost forgotten that name, Rosie. Thomas was the only one who called me that and it endeared him to me.

"I'll catch up with you girls later," he said as he turned and winked at Maggie, who acted like she didn't like it. I knew better. "I have to be getting these fish inside. You two just be off. We've got lots of time, you and me, now that you're home." Thomas looked a bit melancholy as he patted me on the shoulder and headed back to his work.

I headed back to Maggie, who was in the boat, blushing a bit. It was adorable. "Come on Mags, let's head out." I got in the whaler that had a name clumsily hand painted on the side of it. It simply read, "TWINS". I can't think about that today.

"Let's just laze around in the lagoon for today, Maggie. It's been a long time since I've piloted one of these things." My mind drifted momentarily back to my brother. I couldn't help it. I quickly snapped out of it at the sound of the engine lighting up.

Maggie may be in her late 70's, but she's still young at heart! She obviously had other plans than I. After flying across the ocean, we landed at the sandbar that only the Islanders knew of. I loved this place.

As we cut the engine and drift towards this sandbar in the middle of nowhere, the sea is like glass surrounding our private destination. Maggie's the first to leap out of the boat and wade to shore.

I dropped anchor, grabbed the picnic basket and a blanket and held them up high as I made my way to shore. Maggie and I headed toward the other side of the massive sand bar and jump on each step as our feet burn from the fiery sand. On the other side we know is a hot spring and we can't wait to get there.

"This is nice isn't it Maggie," I asked as we sat in the warm, soothing water.

"'Tis wonderful for me achin' bones."

There was a long period of silence before Maggie spoke again. "Sharon, I've been a little angry with you."

"I'm sorry, Maggie. I know. I left you all after Shon's death. I just couldn't stay here. Everything reminds me of him."

"I understand, darlin' but it was hard on everyone. Your parents lost two children that day. They really needed you and you never even called."

"I couldn't. I know it was selfish, but I needed to survive Shon's death and I couldn't do it here."

"What have you been doin' in that big city of yours?"

"I've been doing all the wrong things, Maggie. I pretty nearly drank my life away trying to pretend everything was okay. I wrote a lot. Writing romance novels was just a way of escaping reality."

"I think 'Boat House Beauty' was my favorite," Maggie surprisingly announced.

"Maggie! You read one of my books?! But how..."

"You know how I love the bookstore, Sharon. Well, you're apparently quite famous, because even our little store carries your books. All 4 of them! And, yes, I've read them all. I can't wait to find out what happens to Bridgette in the sequel you're promising," Maggie smiled.

"Oh, Maggie," I cried as I fell into her arms in a puddle of tears.

"There, there, child. I'm not mad at you. I love you. I've just missed you so. Come on, let's have something to eat."

CHAPTER 7

Harbor Help

I decided to take the whaler back into dock and let Maggie rest. It had been a long day already and it was really hot out there. As we came into the harbor I decided to take a swim before docking.

"Hey, Maggie. Wanna take a swim? I promise to watch out for the jelly fish."

"No, not me. I'm afraid my swimming days are over. You go. I'll wait right here in the boat for you. I'm quite content. Stay close," Maggie coddled as she leaned back on her hands and raised her chin just enough to feel the sun's warmth gently caress her face.

"I will," I shouted as I dove off the boat. The water was like a warm bath; almost as warm as the spring on the sandbar. All I need now are some bubbles and a good book.

About ten minutes had passed when I heard Maggie screaming. I was kind of far from her at this point and couldn't really make out what was going on, but I was sure she was in some kind of trouble. So I swam as fast as I could but kept going under the water because I was panicking. Maggie and Thomas are all I have left. All I could think was, "what if I can't get there fast enough."

As I got closer a new fear built inside me as I realized that it was me who was in danger. I can hear Maggie shouting, "SHARK! BEHIND YOU, SHARON! HURRY! IT'S GETTING CLOSER!"

Sharks rarely came into the harbor and if it was here, it was hungry. Maggie tried to start up the boat but couldn't because she was so nervous. So, grabbing the oar she tried with all her might to row closer to me as I swam closer to her. Just then I felt the sharp skin of the shark scrape my leg as it passed by. Terror rose in my throat and I couldn't breathe.

As the shark circled back around, I saw Maggie holding out an oar. "TAKE IT SHARON! GRAB HOLD OF THE OAR! HURRY!" Maggie was trying frantically to pull me into the boat when there came a loud explosion sound.

I was safely in the boat and I turned around just in time to see the size of the fish that had been after me as it stopped suddenly in its pursuit. It began sinking just inches away from the boat in which Maggie and I were now clinging to each other. Maggie shouted as she looked up to Heaven saying, "Thank you, Dear, Sweet Jesus!"

I was in shock as Maggie rocked me and stroked my hair. "You're all I have Sharon. Thank God you're alright!"

Just as we pulled into the dock, Thomas was there to help us out of the boat. "I'd like to know what, in all that is wrong, was a shark doing in the harbor," Thomas managed! "Take Rosie on in the house, Maggie and get her in a hot bath. That'll calm her. I'll tie up the boat."

Thomas has a full head of soft, white, wavy hair and sky blue eyes that reflect years of wisdom. I especially love the crow's feet around his eyes that come from a kind smile.

Once I had my bath and got dressed, I came down to the kitchen for a cup of tea as Thomas recounted the scene for us, which so many had witnessed.

It was the new Sheriff, Sheriff Smallcombe who saved you, Sharon. Thank the Lord he had just finished having lunch on the picnic tables at the Porthole and heard you screaming, Maggie. This is one of those times I'm thankful for your incredible set of lungs, darlin'." He turned to smile at Maggie, playfully as she shot him a look of contempt.

"Alcott, that's the Sheriff's proper name, ran to see what was going on and upon seeing the spectacle, took out his pistol and fired two shots right between the shark's beady eyes!"

I was sickened by the thought of it all, but truly thankful that the sheriff was there when we needed him. Maggie could've been bumped right out of the boat as well! I need to thank that man. But how?

CHAPTER 8

Old and New

Back at the house, while Thomas tended the garden, Maggie was cleaning up the breakfast dishes that we had left behind earlier. I heard a knock at the door so I went to open it. There, before me, stood the most beautiful man I had ever set eyes on. He was 6' tall with broad shoulders and a firm chest. He was wearing a t-shirt that strained to hold in his arms and his jeans fit like they were made just for him. He had a dark, thick head of hair that he wore slightly long and tussled. There was a wave in it that made me want to run my fingers through it. It was his eyes though that captured me. They were light green and contrasted with his dark hair and skin, making it hard to look away. I was totally mesmerized in that moment. I couldn't even speak to invite him in.

Thank God for Maggie. She came to my rescue. Only then did I release the breath I had been holding since the door opened. "Come on in Sheriff," Maggie said to break the spell. "Come in and have a bite. It's the least we can do for you."

They walked right past me as my hand was still holding the door open. All I could do was stare.

Maggie began the introduction, "Sheriff Smallcombe, this here statue is my Sharon."

"It's a pleasure to know you Sharon. I already know Mrs. Mulcahey," said Alcott in his best English accent, which, by the way, made my stomach do flips.

"It's Maggie, Sheriff. Mrs. Mulcahey makes me sound old."

"I'm sorry......Maggie. And it's Alcott if you don't mind." When he smiled you could see the dimples in his cheeks and that made him even more handsome.

I'm feeling like a schoolgirl and having trouble holding back a silly giggle.

"Well Alcott, I just happened to be brewing some good strong Irish tea," Maggie interjected. "Would you care to join us for a cup?"

"I'd love to, Maggie. I've heard from Thomas Daley down at the docks that you make the best cup of tea on the whole Island. I'd feel privileged to join you two beautiful ladies."

He shot a smile with those piercing eyes at me that bore a hole right into my very soul. I couldn't help but blush. And you really knew it when I blushed because my skin was so white. I couldn't believe the spell this man was putting on me; I was never this easily charmed by men before. Men flirt with me all the time. What was different about this guy? He seemed sincere. That was the hook. I was intoxicated by his scent. It was a distinct aroma of clean, crisp, salt air and Dial soap that surrounded him. I liked it. I liked it a lot.

"Don't think I'm being forward Maggie, but you wouldn't be making any of those raisin, cinnamon scones Thomas snags for me from time to time, would you? I thought I smelled something wonderful wafting through the house as I came in," Alcott added playfully.

"Dear God," I thought; "He's still interested in food?!"

"I just took a fresh batch out of the oven," Maggie answered with pride. "Why don't you sit down with us and have a nice long chat. Wouldn't we just love to have the company of a nice gentleman like Alcott with our tea this afternoon, Sharon dear?" Maggie pinched my arm to bring me back.

I wanted to crawl through the wall and become invisible. I couldn't believe Maggie was trying to fix me up with any available man she came across, and so boldly that there's no way the Sheriff didn't see it! I'll get her later for this one, I thought. "Of course Alcott, won't you please make yourself comfortable?" I said while giving Maggie the meanest look I could muster with company watching.

As Alcott took a seat at the kitchen table he said, "You know, there hasn't been a shark around these parts in a long while, not in the harbor, anyway. At least that's what I've seen in the office records. Seeing you struggling in that water today, Sharon made me glad, for once, that I carry a gun."

Maggie took his hand and said tenderly, Sheriff, ya are an angel sent from above, ya are."

Sharon looked at the Sheriff and nodded her head in agreement, trying not to show the emotion that was catching in her throat. "I probably wouldn't be here if you weren't so fast on your feet today. When I think back on it it's even more frightening. I don't know how to thank you." I stood up and went to the counter, bringing back a tray hosting an array of goodies. There were scones, jelly, butter, and clotted cream.

Maggie poured the pot of freshly brewed tea into the awaiting Blue Willow cups. She then looked to Sharon and then to Alcott smiling in her complete content.

Accepting his cup of tea from Maggie, while drinking in Sharon's beauty, Alcott said, "No need to thank me, Sharon. I was just doing my job. I'm just glad it ended up with you both safe and sound. That was a pretty close call and a very big shark. It weighed in at 550 pounds, you know. Sharks love the warm water and it was quite warm today. Adding all the activity in the harbor, since sharks are drawn to noise, I can see how this could've happened. I had to post a sign for no swimming in the harbor for awhile. Sorry ladies."

"That's okay. We know a private area where we can swim pretty safely, away from the crowds, and hopefully sharks," I said just as the doorbell rang.

"Did you ever have one of those dreams," I continued, "where you're running as fast as you can, but you're getting nowhere?"

"Yes, I have," said Alcott attentively.

"That's exactly how it felt when I knew a shark was after me. Like I was swimming with all my might and getting nowhere!"

As Alcott and I continued talking, Maggie came back into the kitchen with yet another guest. I hadn't seen this place so busy since.....well in a long time.

There, in the doorway, between the kitchen and the pantry stood a man I knew, but not as he looked now. The man or the boy I knew before I left the island was a complete nerd. Lanky, pale, wearing thick, dark-rimmed eyeglasses that were made from the bottom of coke bottles and who had a total lack of confidence around girls. This man was about six foot one with sandy blonde hair and deep pools of blue resting in his eyes. A few years and a pair of contact lenses does a body good. Man he looked good!

I awkwardly held out my hand in greeting and said, "Hello, Michael. Or is it Dr. Brennan? It's been awhile."

Alcott was taking all this in and was not liking the connection he was witnessing between me and Dr. Brennan.

Although the sight of Sharon had his heart beating through his chest, Michael managed to smile and said, "No, for you, Sharon, it's still Michael. I was down at the Fisherman's Grille for a cup of chowda when I heard some story about a shark in the harbor today and that you and Maggie were somehow involved. Are you ok? Was anyone harmed? Maybe I should examine you, Sharon." He couldn't help but smile at the thought.

"We're both fine, thank you for asking, Dr.," answered Maggie.

"Come in and we'll tell you all about it. We're having tea and goodies. There's plenty."

Noticing the Sheriff, Michael forced the words from his jealous throat, "Good job, Alcott. I'm forever in your debt. Word around town is you're a hero. Thank you for saving our Sharon." Michael wanted Alcott to feel like an outsider and make him think that Sharon was spoken for.

Confused and not to be outdone, Alcott replied, "Just doing my job, Doc, just doing my job. Maybe you could examine the fish." Then he got up with all the cool he could muster, bent over to kiss Sharon on the cheek and calmly thanked Maggie for her hospitality as he walked away and out the door.

I watched him walk away and the view was just as good going as it was coming.

CHAPTER 9

The Duel

That night I dreamed of two knights dueling for my love. I was the princess and both knights, coincidentally named Sir Alcott of Smallcombe and Sir Michael of Brennan, wanted to marry me. They mounted their trusty steeds. Sir Michael on a white horse and Sir Alcott on his black horse. The two raced towards each other and both men were knocked clear off their prospective horses and came thundering to the ground.

Once on the ground, they drew their swords and began dueling. I watched nervously for I did not want either of them to be hurt. You see, I liked them both equally.

The two men fought and fought until finally, the duel ended and a victor was proclaimed!

I was wakened from this amazing dream by a loud clap of thunder. Thunder scares me to my bones because it was storming the day my brother died. I bolted up in my bed as a flash of lightening lit the room. I realized I was sweating from fear when I got up to close the window. I ran back to my bed, jumped into it and threw the covers over my head. I laid there thinking about my dream and wondering who had won the duel.

After awhile, since I couldn't sleep anyway, I slipped out from under my protective barrier of covers, and crept downstairs to make a pot of tea. Tea always made me feel better.

Maggie was already in the kitchen when I entered. "Mornin', Sharon dear. Can't sleep? Me neither. I figured you'd be up. You always got up when the storms came, even as a child. Tea's ready."

I pushed a hair from my face, and looked at Maggie. "I think tea is just what the Doctor ordered. Thanks, Mags." With that I yawned, stretched and sat down at the table, rubbing my eyes.

"We'll be back to sleep before you know it, child," Maggie touted as she set out the cups and saucers.

"Maggie," I confessed hesitantly, "I just had the silliest dream." I really wanted to tell someone and Maggie had always been a trusted confidant.

It was about Alcott and Michael.

Maggie perked up and leaned in, "Go on dear."

"They were knights and, don't laugh now, they were dueling over my love." I shot a look of warning her way and caught her laughing, quietly.

"I won't be able to look at either one of them again without thinking of that silly dream!"

"Oh, love, that is funny. I'm sorry to laugh, but I'm just giddy at the thought of you wanting love. No wonder you're down here trying to calm down. It must be exciting having two such handsome men fighting over you. You know, your dream isn't that far-fetched. I think that Sheriff has his hat set for ya and was a wee bit jealous of the Doctor paying you a call today. Ya do know that Michael has always been taken with ya."

I laughed at that, because as he was before, it was *never* going to happen!

"Oh, Maggie, they have more to do than think about me. A doctor and a sheriff? They've got better things to do with their time. I'm sure you're mistaken about that. That's funny," I said as I got up to take my cup to the sink. Looking out the window, dreamily, not even noticing the storm now, I said, "Alcott and me. Two people couldn't be further apart. And Michael, well, he's Michael."

CHAPTER 10

One Amazing Day

After going back to bed and getting some sleep, I woke up and looked out my bedroom window. I really love this room because it is surrounded by windows overlooking the harbor. Most people probably wouldn't appreciate being woken up by the sun and seagulls calling, but I love it. The sun was just coming up over the water and the seagulls were making their presence known. I always loved the sight of the sun dancing on the sea like glitter. The first ferry was just coming in port, filled with a new load of tourists.

I went downstairs to have some breakfast. Something about the ocean air always made me ravenous. Maggie, of course, was already setting food out on the table for us. I spoke through mouthfuls of muffins and fruit and bacon. Oh, how I love bacon! "Maggie, I think I'll take the ferry to the mainland today. I need to do some shopping. Would you like to come with me?"

"Well dear, I would, but I promised Thomas that I'd go out with him in his ole fishing boat today. Do you mind terribly? If you need me to go with you...."

I interrupted, "No, Maggie. I'll be fine by myself. You go ahead with Thomas." Truth is, I could use some time alone right now.

"Thank you Sharon, dear. You go and have a good day now," said Maggie.

I found myself, yet again standing on the deck of the ferry, feeling the breeze on my face. I let my mind slip in to a daydream, trying to go back to the duel to see how it would end. I almost forgot where I was until I felt an arm around my waist.

"Good morning, Sharon; please tell me you're not leaving us already."

Startled by my sudden trip back to reality, I turned around and, blinded by the sun, squinted to see who was there. "Oh, Sir Michael, what a nice surprise!"

Michael smiled and said, "Why so formal? Not even my nurse calls me Sir."

I was so embarrassed. My mind was obviously still deep in fantasy land. I scrambled for the right words as I felt the blood rushing back into my blushing cheeks. "Oh, sorry, Michael. I've been reading this romance novel," I lied, "and I guess I'm just engrossed in it."

"No apologies necessary my lady," he said as he took my hand, bent over and kissed it. "I enjoy a good romance myself from time to time. What's the name of the book? Maybe I've read it."

Now I was really on the spot. What was the name of that book I read with the knights in it anyway? "It's funny, I can't seem to remember it off the top of my head. I'll have to get back to you on that one." Note to self, get a romance novel right away and read it!

"I look forward to it, Sharon. Well, in the meantime it just so happens that I'm going to Hyannis today. I'm doing some work around my yard and need to pick up some plants I ordered. It's a hobby of mine. Actually, Thomas taught me pretty much everything I know about gardening. I've got my truck. Could I give you lift?"

Although I had planned on taking a taxi, I must admit this sounded much better. "Thanks, Michael. I think I'll take you up on that offer."

"The ship will be docking soon. Please go to your vehicles now," came the garbled announcement over the loud speaker.

"That's us," said Michael. "We'd better get down below before they block off the stairways."

"Ok. Right behind you."

In the belly of the ferry sat all the parked cars waiting to unload, filled with people from all over. Where were they all going, I wondered. Michael offered his hand to me to help me up into the massive pickup truck. He really was gallant, after all. I love that in a man!

When our hands touched, I can't explain why, but I felt my heart pounding out of my chest. Did he feel it too?

Michael pulled himself up into his seat like he was mounting his trusty steed. I really need to get this dream out of my head!!

"We've missed you on the island, Sharon. I missed you. Every summer I watch the boats come and go and hope to see you. You know I've always liked you. Since we were kids, I've had a huge crush, but was always afraid to tell you. I'm not afraid anymore."

"I like you too, Michael," I said in a sisterly way as I patted his arm. I wasn't ready to let him in yet. After all, I'm not sure how this duel is going to turn out. I smiled at the thought.

Changing the subject quickly, Michael asked, "So, where do you want to go today, Sharon?"

"I need to stock up on some necessities and I was hoping to putter around the Christmas Tree

Shop for awhile. I always loved going there with my Mom."

There was an awkward silence, then Michael continued, "I'm going to Home Depot to get my gardening supplies, so I'll drop you at the Christmas Tree Shop and pick you up when I'm done. Take your time puttering, then we can both do the stock up thing. How's that sound?"

"Sounds perfect. Thanks again."

"It's my absolute pleasure. I can't think of anyone I'd rather spend a day with than you, Sharon Rose Walsh. As long as we're out, why don't we grab some lunch later. We have to eat, right? I know a great new place where we can relax. They even have seats outside overlooking the ocean."

The ferry pulled into port and the vehicles were allowed to disembark. As we were driving off the boat, other cars were already lined up waiting to go on for the return trip. Passengers were standing by the stairway, waiting their turn to enter the ferry and the bicyclists were waiting with the vehicles as well. "It certainly is a busy place," I said.

A little while later we arrived at the Christmas Tree Shop. I was sad and happy all at once, thinking about Mom. Michael got out of the truck, came around my side and opened my door. Again, he took my hand and helped me down. I noticed him checking out my legs as I swung them around to get out of the truck.

As he pulled away I took in a deep breath and thought, "What am I doing?"

CHAPTER 11

A Great Day

As I walked into the store I used to go to with my Mom, a display of dishes caught my eye. They were made of ceramic and had an outdoorsy type of design hand painted on them. The scene held a white picket fence with a gate, birds and flowers on a soft blue background. I could almost see myself living there. Mom would have loved them! She loved everything blue.

I remember when we were kids. Our house was blue from floor to ceiling to couch to walls and everything in between. I guess you could say it was Mom's favorite color. For years I would not allow blue into my life as long as it was my choice. But, somehow, in this moment, I wanted it. I wanted it all.

I grabbed a cart and started loading up. I chose eight place settings, including bowls, dinner plates, salad plates, a huge pasta bowl and, of course the entire tea set, pot, sugar, creamer and tray. The tea pot hat a blue bird singing for a spout. I also found a napkin holder, butter dish and the tea cups and saucers. It was an impulse buy, but I felt closer to Mom in that moment and really needed that.

I helped the cashier wrap every single item for the trip, realizing they would be having a bumpy ride back in the pickup.

After standing outside for about ten minutes, Michael arrived. He pulled right up to me and laughed, seeing my full carriage. "This is browsing?" he said sarcastically.

"It could've been worse. I could've gotten the ultra-deluxe sized gas grill they were pushing," I laughed.

"Here, let me help you, Sharon," Michael said as he emptied my carriage into his truck with as much grace as an elephant on roller skates. Then he rushed to help me up into the truck just as I was opening the door.

"The restaurant I mentioned is over in Yarmouth, Sharon. It's only about ten minutes away, depending on traffic, of course. I hope you're hungry? The portions are enormous."

I looked at him and thought, *"Your eyes are enormous!"* "You may be horrified at the amount of food I can put away, Michael."

The song, *"Love Can Build A Bridge"* by the Judd's was playing on the radio as we drove. I used to sing that with my Mom. Why does everything here have to remind me of my family? This is exactly why I hadn't been back for so long.

A few minutes later I saw the sign for the restaurant. "There's the restaurant, Michael. You did say 'The Gull', right?"

Michael squinted and looked up ahead, "Wow, you've got great eyes, Sharon. I can barely make that out from here. I guess it's time for a checkup."

"No, it's probably not you, Michael. I had laser surgery on my eyes to correct my vision a couple of years ago and now I seem to have super human eyesight. It's pretty cool."

Once seated inside I found myself checking Michael out again. I never realized how handsome he was. Well, probably because he wasn't last time I saw him. 'He's aging nicely,' I thought.

"Can I get you a drink, Miss," asked the waiter for the second time, with as much patience as he could muster?

"Oh, I'm sorry. I would like a decaf iced tea with a twist of lemon please."

"And for the gentleman?"

"I'll have the same. Thank you." He was looking at me as he ordered and said, "Penny for your thoughts."

"I was just thinking about how nice it is to be here."

"I'm so glad you came home, Sharon. I hope you stay for awhile....forever." He looked down and cleared his throat in an attempt to gain his composure.

I found myself at a loss for words for the first time in my life. I thought it best to just pretend it didn't happen. "You've been here before, Michael. Do you know what you want?"

He knew what he wanted. I could see it in his eyes.

"Well I know what I want," I continued nervously. "I'll have a king cut of prime rib, medium, a baked potato with all the fixings, some asparagus and a bowl of clam chowder. That triple chocolate cake looks amazing. I think I want a hunk of that to take home. I'll get one for Maggie too."

"Wow! You were right. I am horrified," Michael laughed. I love lobster and I haven't had it in awhile, so I'm getting that. Oh, wait they have twin on special. Two is definitely better than one. Baked Potato with sour cream and shrimp cocktail. None of those pesky vegetables for me. I do want to bring home their strawberries and cream. It's amazing! The strawberries are the biggest, juiciest, sweetest berries you will ever have. If you're good, maybe I'll share."

The lunch came as we talked over old times. Michael's lobster kept squirting me in the face as he tore at it, but I didn't care because he gave me the claws; my favorite part. I took one of them and tried to crack it open with the nutcracker, but my hands were slippery from the last one and it flew right out of my hands and into Michael's lap.

We got quiet suddenly as the tension seemed to build. "Oh, I'm so sorry," I laughed. "Let me help you."

"No, I'm fine. It's not a problem, really."

I dipped my napkin in some lemon water and knelt down beside Michael in an attempt to clean him up. I could feel his warm breath on my neck and when I looked up, our eyes met. Michael lifted my chin and kissed me gently. It was tender and I liked it. He had such soft lips. I liked it too much. I got up and went back to my seat. I can't get involved. I have a life back in Boston. I have no intention of staying.

CHAPTER 12

Dancing

By the time we finished running all our errands it was early evening. We ate so much lunch that we didn't really need any dinner.

"Hey, Sharon, do you want to go over to the Irish Village for a drink? We have plenty of time before we have to catch the last ferry."

"I haven't been there since my Dad took me dancing on my 16th Birthday. Are you sure we have time?" I was elated at the thought of going there again. I knew, somehow, that I'd be able to feel my father's spirit on that dance floor.

Michael paid the check. As we got up from the table to leave, he put his arm around my waist and said, "You just relax, you're on vacation and we have plenty of time." It felt nice to be taken care of. I've been on my own for so long.

As we walked into the famed Irish Village, I could hear the song "The Wild Rover" being played by the band. We sat at a table right beside the dance floor and immediately our feet started tapping to the music. The energy of the Irish music made me want to get up and move to it.

The waitress came over and said, "Good evening. What can I get you?"

"Yes, we'd like two Irish coffees, please," Michael assumed. "Oh, and a couple of onion tarts." Then, looking over at me, he nodded as if to ask, "Is that ok?"

I nodded back.

As we ate our onion tarts, which, by the way were amazing, we watched others dance. Then the band played "Danny Boy." I couldn't hold back the tears. Thomas sang that song at Shon's funeral. I swear if they start playing bagpipes, I'll be reduced to a puddle.

Michael took my hand and without a word, wiped the tears from my eyes with his napkin. I didn't mind that it smelled like onions. Then he guided me to the dance floor.

We moved together as if we were one. Letting my inhibitions go I rested my head on his chest and just let the tears flow. For some reason I couldn't explain I felt safe with Michael. He stood back a little so he could look into my eyes. Again, he kissed me. This time he lingered, just a little.

It suddenly became evident that the music had stopped and we were alone in the middle of the dance floor. We didn't care what anyone else thought so we walked back to our table arm in arm.

When we had finished our second round of Irish coffees, it was time to drive back to the ferry. Neither one of us wanted the night to end. When we came out of the Irish Village, it was pouring rain and incredibly windy.

Arriving at the pier, the parking lot was jammed with cars. Just as we thought. All boats were being cancelled for the rest of the night due to high wind conditions. I knew we should've just gone straight back after our errands. That's what I get for letting my guard down.

Michael said, "Looks like we're stuck off Island for tonight, Sharon. I hope you're okay with that. Let's see if we can find a place to stay back in Hyannis. There isn't any sense looking around here with this traffic. I'm sure the hotels in this area are booked already."

"You're right. We won't find anywhere to stay here. Can I use your cell phone to call Maggie? I left mine back at the house. She'll be worried by now. I'm sure she's been watching the skies and listening to that scanner of hers."

As he handed me his phone he said, "Yeah, I'd better notify my service that I won't be back until tomorrow. Dr. Sanderson will cover for me."

I was a little concerned about spending the night away with him in the same hotel, but it will be fine in separate rooms, anyway. We've been getting along and maybe a little too close, but I'm sure it'll be fine.

We drove back to Hyannis and kept a close eye out for any signs of vacancy on hotels and motels. We found lots of "NO VACANCY" signs so far. We had to drive all the way to the Red Jacket in Yarmouth before we found a place. The clerk there told us that they only had one room left. We had no choice but to take it or sleep in the truck and that wasn't happening. So we took it.

We turned the key, opened the door and there, smack dab in the middle of the room stood the one and only bed. It may as well have had neon signs pointing to it saying *"RIGHT THIS WAY"*, *"STEP RIGHT UP"*, *"DON'T BE SHY"!!* But what I was thinking was more like, *"STOP!"*, *"PROCEED WITH CAUTION!"*, *"DO NOT ENTER!"* Talk about pressure!

CHAPTER 13

What Now?

Michael was standing in front of the window, sun shining on him when I woke up. He seemed so peaceful and I just wanted to drink in the view. This man in whom I never gave a second thought, was now wrapped up in my every thought. I wondered how he could look so good after sleeping in the bathtub with nothing but a blanket and pillow all night.

He must've heard me stir because he slowly turned towards me, hands in his pockets and said, "Good morning, Sharon. I gather you slept well."

"I did. I'm very surprised about that because I never sleep through storms."

"Well I can tell you one thing," Michael offered. "You snore like a truck driver!"

"I do not! Take that back!" I was horrified.

Michael was laughing hysterically. "You're so adorable when you're mad. I didn't know before last night that someone could actually out snore the sound of thunder crashing through walls!"

"I don't snore, Michael! You're just being mean!"

"Okay, okay. I take it back. You don't snore. You're a perfect little princess without any bodily functions. In fact, you probably don't even need to use the bathroom, right?" Michael teased.

Then, changing the subject so I couldn't rebut, "Hey, I'm hungry," he added. "Why don't you take your time getting up and showered while

I get us something to eat. Take your time. I'll be back."

And with that he kissed me on the forehead and left the room.

Hours passed without a sign of Michael. I was starting to worry. I looked outside to see if his truck was in the lot, but it wasn't. Just then the phone rang and it startled me. I ran over to it and picked it up, fully expecting it to be Michael.

"This is Officer Sweeney from the Hyannis Police Department," the voice on the phone began. My heart caught in my throat. Something was wrong and I knew it.

"Michael Brennan has been in an accident with his vehicle and has been transported to Cape Cod Hospital in Hyannis."

"Is he okay," I asked not yet realizing the severity of the accident.

"Ma'am, all I'm able to tell you at this time is that he is injured and unconscious. I don't know the extent of the injuries and I'm not at liberty to give personal information to anyone except immediate family. Are you family?"

"No, no I'm not," I said as I hung up the phone without saying goodbye. I was numb. It's never good when they talk about immediately family or won't tell you how he is.

In somewhat of a fog I managed to pick up the phone and call the front desk to request a cab. It seemed like a lifetime before they arrived. "Cape Cod Hospital, please," came the halfhearted request from the back seat.

"Okay. It's none of my business but, are you alright," the cab driver asked?

"Mhm," was all I said as he drove on. I stared out the car window as we moved at a snail's pace through all the traffic. What would I say when I got there? I'm not family. Will they let me see him? I have to find a phone and call Maggie. I have to get his truck for him. Okay, one thing at a time. Michael first.

When I arrived at the hospital I was informed that Michael had been taken to the ICU. I went there immediately to see him. "Which room is Michael Brennan in," I asked the desk clerk?

She looked at her computer screen then at me and asked, "Are you a relative?"

What was she reading on that screen? How bad was it? I almost didn't want to know. I had let him get so close to me so fast, that it felt like he was mine already.

Thinking quick on my feet as I always did, and knowing I would not be allowed past the 'guard' if I was not a relative, I lied. "Yes, I'm Michael's younger sister, Sharon."

"Okay," came the trusting nurse's reply. "You may go right in; but only for a few minutes. He's pretty badly hurt. And, Miss, I need to prepare you, it's a difficult sight to take in."

Slowly opening the door to his room, I approached the bed. He was hooked up to so many machines; some were beeping and others had blips on the screen, he had an IV and a bag dripping through tubes into him and his body.... His poor, beat up body had casts and braces all over. I could barely see him through it all.

"Michael?"

He didn't respond to my voice and his eyes were closed. I didn't even recognize his once beautiful face! Why do terrible things always happen to people I love?!

"Oh, Michael," I cried. "Wake up! Oh, please wake up." The sight of all of this was too much to bear.

There was no response. There was no movement. There was only the sound of the machines blipping to the rhythm of his precious heartbeat.

That's when the doctor came in and I asked him, "Is he going to be alright, Doctor?"

"The nurse said you are his sister. Is that correct, Miss," asked the Doctor?

"Yes, that's right." I kept the lie going. I looked at Michael and knew I would not leave him in this place alone. No one was going to pull me away. I couldn't let him be alone when he opened his eyes.

"I'm sorry, Miss..."

"Sharon. My name is Sharon. Is he going to be okay, Doctor?"

"I'm sorry, I can't answer that yet. It's all up to him right now. He has to have a reason to live. He's in a coma. I don't know when or if he will come out of it."

The tears were burning my face now, and they silently rolled down my cheeks as the doctor rambled on. I couldn't even listen anymore. Why was he talking to me anyway? *"Do Something,"* I screamed inside my head as my body crumbled!

"You see all these machines in this room, Sharon? They are breathing for him right now. He's been hurt pretty badly. There were multiple contusions to his head, his skull has been cracked, his legs are both broken and he has three broken ribs. All of these components together are making it quite difficult for him to breathe on his own. Even if he does come out of the coma, he may have permanent brain damage. I'm sorry. I'm truly sorry."

After giving me what felt like a nanosecond to take all that in he told me his name and informed me that he would be tending to Michael at night if I had any more questions. Dr. Shapiro. I won't remember that past the next minute.

"Thank you. I do have a question now though, if you don't mind. Do you know what happened?"

"From what the police told me, an oil truck hit him head on. Mr. Brennan's vehicle is totaled. You can pick up his belongings at the police station."

Dr. Shapiro started to leave the room, then turned back around, paused for a moment and then, looking thoughtful added, "I'm a man of science not of faith, but for the life of me I can't explain how he survived the crash."

CHAPTER 14

Visiting Hours

Three weeks went by and still no sign of life from Michael. I had gone home when his parents arrived and buried my parents. That was the reason I was here. It was a small, quiet funeral that was held in our back yard where our family burial plot lay. They were laid to rest right next to Shon, overlooking the ocean.

I packed up some clothes and necessities and moved into a hotel nearest the hospital so I could be close to Michael.

His parents, Ida and Ken made the trip off island as often as possible. I picked them up at the boat so they wouldn't have to pay to bring their car over and I brought them home late in the afternoon. I would then go back to the hospital and stay with Michael until visiting hours were over.

Maggie and Thomas were regular visitors as well. After about a week, I told the staff that I was not Michael's sister, but by then they had already figured it out and allowed me to stay at Ida's request.

On Saturday, twenty-three days after the accident, I was in the cafeteria of the hospital having coffee when I looked up and saw Alcott walking towards me. "Mind if I sit down," he asked? I wondered why the Sheriff was here.

"Alcott," I said, surprised. "What are you doing here?"

"I came to see you. Do you need anything? Are *you* okay? I heard about Michael but wanted to give you some time before I came over. Maggie's worried sick about you. She wants you to come home. It's not healthy for you to be here every day. Are you eating? You don't look like you've been eating, Sharon." He reached for my hand across the table. I barely knew this man.

"I will admit, Alcott," I began as I pulled my hand back, "I have been feeling pretty lousy the last few days. I'm really run down since the accident. I haven't been getting much sleep either. I can't help but blame myself for this. Maybe if I had gone with him to get breakfast..."

"Maybe I should go home for a couple of days, but how can I leave Michael? What if he wakes up and no one is here?"

"Michael's parents are here and we can ask the doctor to call you if there are any changes. Michael wouldn't want you here if he knew you were sick. Just to be safe though, let's ask the doctor to look at you."

"I'm fine. I'm just overtired, that's all."

"Just the same, I'll feel better if we get a professional opinion. Come on or I'll have to carry you. You wouldn't want that would you," smiled Alcott trying to lighten my mood?"

"Okay, Alcott, I'll go; but it's silly. I'm fine, really."

Dr. Shapiro examined me while asking questions and took a blood sample to check for Mononucleosis and anemia. "It'll take a little while to get the results back. I'm checking a couple of things to see if there's a reason for your fatigue. You probably just aren't taking care of yourself. I wouldn't worry about it. I'll call you in awhile."

"Thanks Doc, for everything. I'm going up to check on Michael, now."

I went back up to the room with Alcott in tow. He was allowed in purely because he was an officer of the law.

Leaning over I gave Michael a kiss on the cheek and said, "Hey! I brought you a visitor. Maggie's a worrywart so she sent him over here to check on us."

"Hi Michael! It's Alcott. Hey, why don't you stop faking it and get up. You're going to miss the fishing derby and I need a partner that knows the waters like you do," said Alcott. Nothing. "Okay, then, I'll go back home, get the boat all gassed up and wait for you. See you soon, buddy."

Alcott and Michael had become close in the last year and were regular fishing buddies.

"I'll just let Michael know I'm leaving and I'll meet you outside, Alcott."

"Okay, Sharon. Take your time."

Ida and Ken were still by Michael's side so I told them I was going back home with Alcott for a couple of days. "Please call me, Ida if there is any change at all. If he flutters an eyelash I want to know about it. Here's the key to my hotel room and a key to my car. You two can use them while I'm gone."

I leaned over and kissed Michael goodbye. I didn't care who saw me. Then I whispered in his ear, "I love you."

CHAPTER 15

A True Friend

After leaving the hospital Alcott drove me to the hotel to pick up a few things. The hotel took care of my laundry, but I wanted to change it out for some other clothes and maybe bring back some healthy food to keep on hand.

Alcott had reservations for his car so it was easy to board the ferry. I didn't have to carry my luggage or anything, just drive on. We parked then went to the top deck to enjoy the cool night air.

"I'm going to get us something to eat, Sharon," said Alcott. "I'll be right back."

As he walked away I cried and cried. Those were the last words Michael had said to me. I pulled myself together just as Alcott came back.

"I wasn't sure how you took your coffee so I put the cream and sugar on the side. I hope you like mustard."

Alcott was handing me a hotdog when I got up and made a beeline for the ladies room. I never got seasick before... why was I feeling so sick? I patted my face with a cold, wet paper towel and headed back to the bow deck.

"Sharon, are you alright? You are white as a sheet. Come sit down."

"I'm sure it's just nerves. I'll be fine. Sorry about that. Would you mind terribly if I don't eat that," I asked as I pointed to the offending food?

"Don't worry about it, Sharon. I can eat both myself, no problem. After I do that, I'm going to get you some ginger ale and crackers. It will settle your stomach."

"I'm sorry to be such a bother."

"I assure you, you are no bother." I almost gagged as I watched him shove two thirds of the first hotdog down his throat.

I took in a deep breath of the fresh sea air and slowly released it. Alcott was back with ginger ale pretty quick and I sipped it slowly while intermittently nibbling on the crackers. I was feeling better.

I still had some crackers left so I tossed them to the hungry gulls floating overhead. I always loved feeding them.

Alcott drove a 1995, anniversary edition of the Ford Mustang. It was midnight black with a black convertible top and cream colored leather seats. I loved that it was a stick. I learned to drive a standard on an old, powder blue VW Beetle that belonged to my mother.

There were so many cars disembarking and so many more waiting to load. Not too long afterward I arrived home. Alcott put the car in park and looked over at me. He took my hand again and asked, "Are you going to be ok? Can I get you anything at the store?"

"You've done so much for me already. It seems like ever since I met you, you've been coming to my rescue. I'm fine, really. I just need some rest."

"Well, I insist on carrying your luggage to the door anyway, Sharon. Don't argue."

"Thanks."

He walked me to the door, handed the suitcase to Thomas who was waiting when we got there and was saying his goodbyes when Maggie came crashing past Thomas.

"Come in the both of ya. I've got a hot pot of tea brewing. I'll not take no for an answer, Sheriff. Get on in here."

"You better listen to her," said Thomas. "She doesn't give in easy."

We went into the kitchen and sat down. I was teary, so Alcott took out a clean, white handkerchief and dried my eyes.

I took it from him and blew my nose in it. Then smiling, I handed it back. "You're a really good friend. Thank you."

"Oh, no. Keep it. It's yours. You never know when you may need one again," Alcott said, not wanting to touch the wretched thing.

"Did anyone call from the hospital, Maggie," I asked?

"No darling, not yet. But they will, don't you be worrying ya'rself. Any day now, they'll call and Michael will be asking for ya."

"I'm tired," I said. "I don't mean to be rude, but I'd like to go to my room now if you don't mind."

"Not at all; that's why you're home, to get some rest. I'll come by and check on you in the morning. If you need anything, give me a call and I'll pick it up on my way over. Bye Maggie; take care of our girl now."

Again he was using Michael's lines.

"You know I will. Thanks for bringing her home."

I slept straight through the night without getting up and didn't even wake up until two o'clock the following afternoon. I was famished.

Maggie informed me there had been a phone call from the hospital a few minutes ago.

"Michael?"

"No, it's not Michael. No changes there yet. It was a Dr. Shapiro. He says you need to call him back about your test results. What test would that be, Sharon dear?"

"It's probably nothing. Dr. Shapiro was testing me for mono because I've been so tired and sick the last few days. I'm sure he just wants to tell me to get some rest."

I called the hospital and was told that I have the flu. They gave me the usual speech about plenty of fluids and rest. That was all no big deal, but I knew I couldn't visit Michael until I felt better because I was contagious. It was going to be a difficult week. I was weak as a kitten and I guess I just needed to be forced into resting.

Alcott came back around four o'clock as promised to check in on me. "You're looking a little better,

Sharon. I guess you were right, you just needed some rest. You are a bit pale though. Can I get you anything?"

"No, I'll be fine, Alcott, but if I were you I wouldn't come too close. I have the flu and trust me, you don't want it."

A couple of days later and a lot of TLC from Maggie I was feeling a lot better. Alcott checked up on me again; why I don't know, but Maggie seemed to really enjoy his company, as did Thomas. I'd be up in my room under Maggie's orders to rest and hear all kinds of uproarious laughter coming from downstairs. Alcott was easy to get along with and it seemed, that once he became a friend, he was there for it all, good and bad. Friends like that are rare.

I worked my way to the back deck for some fresh air, where I found

Maggie, Thomas and Alcott shooting the breeze. "Sharon, dear," said Maggie as I came outside and sat in one of the Adirondack chairs, "We were just talking about going to the Ocean View for dinner tonight if you're up to it."

"That sounds great," I said. All I had eaten lately was soup and crackers with the occasional dry toast and tea. I was so up for a real meal. "And, since you've all taken such good care of me lately, it's on me."

"I wouldn't hear of it, Sharon," said Alcott. "A woman never pays when I'm at the table. My mother brought me up better than that. I'd love to join you, but I'm paying or I'm not going."

How gallant, I thought. Did men like this still really exist? I mean he did hold my car door open for me, but so did Michael. Two *knights* in one place? Maybe it wasn't a dream.

"I'll make six o'clock reservations for us," Maggie said. "That is, if it's alright for a woman to pick up a heavy telephone and make a reservation."

"That'll be great, Maggie," Alcott said with a wink. "So, I'll pick you all up around 5:30?"

We arrived at the Ocean View in Oak Bluffs right on time and were seated almost immediately. I guess being the Sheriff has its perks. I wasn't much in a celebratory mood with Michael out of reach and out of touch, but I knew I needed this time for me.

Alcott got the Chicken Cordon Bleu, which is usually my favorite, but my stomach was still a bit off, so I was going easy on the heavy food. The sauce on that chicken is its own food group. Maggie and Thomas got lobster and I got some lobster corn chowda.

We had a great time and they were all so curious about life in Boston, and Alcott was especially insistent on an answer to the question of how long I was staying on the island. I really had no immediate plans right now. As a writer, I can write anywhere. My heart was fast becoming part of this place again.

After the chowda and conversation I was feeling better and hungry for something other than soup, so I ordered some steamers, dripping in butter and some grilled garlic bread for dipping. It tasted like pure Heaven.

After that size meal, everyone decided to take a walk around the harbor. We walked around the dock, looking at all the boats with their lights on and hearing bits and pieces of people's conversations as they sat in their boats with friends. I always liked looking to see where they had all come from.

We walked to Circuit Ave., which Islanders usually call Circus Ave. because of all the activity on that street. It's really a hot point in Oak Bluffs. Many of the finest gift shops are there and night clubs as well. If you ventured around the corner, you could go into the pizza place for a slice to go in your bare feet!

We went into a few shops, playing the tourist game and picked up some trinkets. We came to "The Carousel" where you could get pretty much any kind of homemade ice cream you could dream up, including lobster ice cream which I have yet to brave a taste of. My absolute favorite is the coconut ice cream on a giant waffle cone.

We all got these huge cones knowing we would not be able to finish them and headed back towards the restaurant where Alcott's car would be waiting.

Back at home, getting Thomas and Maggie out of the back seat of the car was a riot. The classic, 1965, Ford Mustang that Alcott had inherited from his father was so low to the ground that they had to heave ho each other out the door. I'm sure it was rude, but I couldn't stop laughing. I was enjoying being here, with these people.

Yes, I will stay. . . for now.

CHAPTER 16

Good News!

I was awakened by a telephone call at one o'clock in the morning from Michael's mother. He was awake and he was calling my name! The first ferry wouldn't be leaving the island for five more hours. I feel like diving head first into the harbor and swimming over to Falmouth. Six o'clock can't come fast enough. "I'll get there as soon as I can, Ida. Thank you so much for the call!" I didn't even wait for a reply before I hung up the phone and ran upstairs to pack a bag.

I threw anything and everything into my suitcase, left a note for Maggie and ran out the door. I jumped in my car and drove to Alcott's house. Banging on the door, it took a lifetime for him to answer.

Sleepily, he opened the door. "Sharon! What's wrong?"

"Nothing's wrong, Alcott. Everything is great, just great!"

"Then I don't get it. Why are you here at," he pried his eyes open to look at the clock on the wall, "One forty-five in the morning?!"

"Michael is out of his coma! I'm on my way to see him!"

"Oh, that's great news, Sharon, but you do know the ferry doesn't run for almost four more hours."

"I know. That's why I'm here. You're the sheriff. You must have a connection with someone who could give me a ride to the mainland," I pleaded.

"Even if I did, Sharon, I couldn't wake them up in the middle of the night. What am I supposed to say, 'It's a matter of life and love?'"

"Please, Alcott. Say anything, just please get me over there. If you don't I swear I'll take the whaler over myself."

"No! It's not safe to do that at night and you know it! Come in. Let me at least put some clothes on and I'll make a call. Jimmy's not going to be happy about this."

I hadn't even realized that Alcott had been standing in the doorway in only a pair of pajama bottoms.

"Help yourself to whatever you want in the kitchen."

Alcott went upstairs which gave me a chance to check out his house. It was small, but cozy. I especially liked the stone fireplace which had seashells and sea glass scattered throughout. In the kitchen I snooped through his cabinets and refrigerator to find that he must be quite a cook. The cabinets were stocked like a professional pantry and the fridge had everything from brie to quail eggs.

I found some leftovers and tugged into them ravenously while sitting on the couch. Good stuff. I was guzzling down a grape soda when Alcott came in. I had pasta sauce dripping down my chin and soda splashed on my t-shirt. It wasn't pretty. "Hungry?"

I wiped my face on my arm and finished swallowing. "I hope you don't mind."

"Not at all. Could I get you anything else? A trough perhaps?"

Changing the subject, "Did you get a hold of your friend, Jimmy," Alcott?

"Jimmy.... Well, let's just say, isn't available this morning. I've got a backup plan. Come on."

Down at the docks Alcott took my suitcase and carried it to the boat he got for me. I couldn't believe my eyes. "Thomas!" Then to Alcott, "You woke up Thomas?!"

Thomas cut in, "No one woke me, Rosie, I always go out on my fishing trips around 2:30am. I like to get a jump on the younger guys and get the best fish. Alcott gave me a call and here we are."

"I don't want you taking me across the ocean, Thomas, it's not safe."

"Are you calling me old, lass?"

"No, Thomas. I just...." It was futile to argue with Thomas, I knew that my whole life. "Thank you, Thomas."

Thomas took my hand and helped me in the fishing boat and to my surprise, Alcott stepped in behind me.

"It's a beautiful morning for a boat ride," Alcott said and sat down. I knew he was coming to be sure

Thomas made it safely back home and I was so thankful.

By the time I arrived at the hospital, Michael was talking up a storm and asking his mother questions about the accident. He didn't appear to have any brain damage. *"Thank you, Jesus. Thank you for answering our prayers."*

He was smiling as much as he could through all the stitches on his beautiful face. I ran to him and held him as tenderly as I could through all the cords and casts.

"Sorry Hon," Michael began. "I hope you'll take a rain check on breakfast. I was on my way to pick it up when I got lost."

"Oh, Michael," I cried. "I've missed you so much."

"How did you get here at this time in the morning, Sharon," asked Ken?

"It's a long story," I said. "I'm just so glad to be here, now."

"It's good to see you, sweetie," Michael said. "Hey, Doc says I'll be good as new. He's going to fix me up with some fancy plastic surgeon who promises I'll look like Mel Gibson when he's done with me. Or would you prefer Tom Cruise?"

"I prefer you."

CHAPTER 17

A Bright Light

I was curious. I had never known anyone who had been in a coma before. "What was it like, Michael? Being in a coma? Could you hear me talking to you, or feel me holding your hand? What did you see in there?"

"It was weird," Michael began. "I was talking to you and you were crying like I couldn't hear you. I was getting frustrated and would yell, 'Yes, I can hear you Sharon! I'm fine!' but you didn't respond."

"You could hear me?"

"Yeah, and I could feel you stroking my hand. I could hear your lovely voice and it made me stay."

"What do you mean, 'stay', Michael?"

"Well, I kept seeing this light ahead of me, and at the end of the light was a crowd of people who seemed to be calling to me with their motions, although I didn't hear them. Then there was you. Right here next to me. So determined to talk to me, that I couldn't ignore you. I could hear and feel you, but I could see them. Your will was so strong that I kept feeling the need to stay and listen to what you were saying. You said you loved me. Did I dream that?"

I was caught off guard. I didn't know he heard that. I wouldn't have had the courage to say it if I knew he was listening. "You weren't dreaming, Michael," I said shyly, with my head down.

Michael took my chin in his hand and raise my face to look at him. I slowly raised my eyes as he said, "I love you too, Sharon." I just smiled. I'll never forget this moment.

Ken and Ida had been standing in the doorway in awe of the story they just witnessed unfolding in this hospital room. They hadn't realized that Michael could have died. It never crossed their minds. Their faith was strong. They were in shock, standing there with the coffees in their hands, unable to speak.

"Mom, Dad," Michael said, noticing them standing there as if stunned by ghostly visions. "Come on in. Did you find something to eat?"

Snapping out of it, Ida quickly said, "Yes, Michael dear, some nurses gave us a few bagels and we got coffee from the vending machine. This should tide us over 'til the cafeteria opens." Then, handing a coffee to Sharon, "Here you go, black, no sugar, right?"

"Yes, thank you Ida. Why don't you come in and visit with Michael for awhile. All this excitement is getting me a little lightheaded. I'm going to get some fresh air. I'll be back shortly, sweetie. You be good now, and don't be harassing the nurses," I said to Michael on my way out.

I started down the hall to the courtyard when I got another dizzy spell and a terrible headache. Next thing I knew I was on a gurney in a hallway and Dr. Shapiro was bent over me.

"What's going on, Dr. Shapiro? How did I get here? This is the weirdest flu I've ever had. It comes and goes. I was fine, then suddenly felt dizzy."

"You passed out in the hallway, Sharon. The nurse called me right away," said Dr. Shapiro. "I'm afraid there may be something more going on than just a flu. I want you to have some tests."

"Not now," I protested.

"Yes, now."

Dr. Shapiro was serious and he was scaring me.

"Nurse, I want an EKG and an MRI, stat! Call me when you're done."

"Right away Doctor," said the nurse as she went to set up the tests.

"Sharon," started Doctor Shapiro. "I don't want to worry you, but there are a couple of other things that could be going on with you. Is it possible that you are pregnant?"

"No! Absolutely not."

"Well, like I said, I don't want to worry you, so let's take the tests first and then discuss the findings. Maybe you do just have a really bad flu bug coupled with exhaustion."

The nurse came back and wheeled Sharon down the hall on the gurney.

"I can walk," I said. I felt silly being treated like an invalid.

"I'm the doctor, and I say you need it. Now, don't fight me on this one. I can't take the chance that you'll faint again and possibly get hurt this time. Nurse Sarah is in charge. I wouldn't mess with her if I were you."

About an hour later, Dr. Shapiro showed up with my test results. I was worried about Michael, but they told me that he was told I was just resting for awhile. The doctor didn't look happy, and that worried me.

"Hi, Sharon. How are you feeling?"

"I'm fine, can I go now? I need to check on Michael."

"He's fine. Let's talk about you."

I became quite frightened at his demeanor as he sat on the side of my bed. "What is it Doc? Just come out with it. You're scaring me!"

"Alright, Sharon. Here it is. You have a tumor resting on your brain. This is causing the dizziness and fainting. The nausea is a side effect of the dizziness and the headache is from vomiting. Stress headache, we call it."

I was stunned. I didn't believe it. "You're mistaken. I think you're looking at the wrong tests. Look again."

"They're not wrong, Sharon. I've been over and over them. This is what we are dealing with and we will get through it together. I have the best staff waiting for you in Boston and the helicopter is on its way."

"What? Wait! What?! What are you saying? I'm not going anywhere."

"Sharon," Dr. Shapiro spoke softly, but firmly. "You can't wait. You have a small, thin tumor wrapped around part of your brain. It has to be removed right away and tested."

"Tested? Tested for what? Cancer?"

"Yes, Sharon. It has to be tested for cancer. I'm not the expert on this subject, but there is a highly skilled team of doctors in Boston that are going to take way better care of you than I can." Then taking my hand in his, "Please, Sharon, you have to do this now. Do you understand what I'm telling you?"

How could this have happened? I've done everything right. I go to the gym six days a week and eat only clean foods and I'm a good person. Why am I being punished?

I just nodded my head.

"I'll tell Michael."

CHAPTER 18

Major Surgery

Twelve hours of surgery had passed and three hours of recovery I was told when I came to. I opened my eyes and saw Maggie first, then Thomas, then Alcott. I felt very weak, so I didn't talk, I just blinked a couple of times to get them in focus. I think I fell asleep a couple of times too.

"Doctor says ya're alright, love," said Maggie, patting my hand. "They got it all. He'll explain to ya later. Thomas called Michael a wee bit ago and he sends his love to ya."

The next time I woke up a doctor was standing beside me. "Hello, Miss Walsh, I'm Dr. Carlton. I performed your surgery with Dr. Statler. How are you feeling?"

"Tired," I managed in my weakened state.

"That's good, Miss Walsh. You're going to need a lot of rest in order to allow your cells to rejuvenate. Now, let me tell you a bit about what's going on with you. We were able to retrieve the entire tumor. It was wrapped around a part of your brain pretty well, but we got it. We sent it off to the lab for testing and will know more as you recover. Now I don't want you to get out of this bed or try to talk too much in the next 48 hours. Ok?"

I nodded, then fell back to sleep.

The next thing I remember was waking up feeling hungry.

"Hi Rosie!" said Thomas when I opened my eyes. "How ya doing, girl?"

"I'm hungry."

He laughed. "You're hungry," then to Maggie, "She's hungry."

Maggie was on the other side of the bed. "Ya've been in and out of sleep for days, Sharon. It's good ta see ya awake."

I was able to sit up and have a meal. It was chicken soup and a roll with juice, ginger ale and green gelatin. It wasn't much to write home about, but it felt good going down.

The doctor came in soon after I finished eating. "I heard you were up. That's good, Sharon. Very good. How do you feel? Any pain, nausea, headaches?"

"No. I feel pretty good. Can I go home?"

"Hold on there. You just got up. We need to observe you for a few more days, then we'll talk."

I pouted a little but was grateful for feeling as well as I did.

"I need to fill you in on the pathology report." Then, turning towards Maggie and Thomas, "Could we have a minute, please?"

"No," I said. "They can stay. They're family."

I saw a tear in Maggie's eye. I don't think I had ever called them that before, but I had known them both my whole life and now they were all I had.

"Alright, then," the doctor began. "As I told you before, we were able to get the whole tumor out. There is not one speck of it left and the possibilities of it coming back are pretty slim. The tests show that the tumor was benign."

"Benign," Thomas said. "That means it's cancer or it's not cancer?"

"It's not cancer. Sharon is going to be just fine. So, I'd say you can probably take her home sometime this weekend." He patted me on the leg and left the room.

I broke down with relief. Maggie being the ever strong presence in my life put on a good front. "See, I told ya. All this fuss for nothing. Well, Thomas, take me home so I can make some decent food for our Sharon and get her some clothes to come home in."

"Yes, dear," Thomas joked.

"We love you. We'll see you soon. Now get some rest," said Maggie.

Thomas kissed me on the cheek and left with her.

Alone in the room I thanked God for allowing me to get through this and stay around awhile longer and I asked Him to heal Michael and make his recovery an easy one.

Just as I was finishing my prayer I heard a familiar voice talking to

Thomas in the hall. Then, walking into my room . . .

"Michael!!" I couldn't get out of bed with all the hookups but I wanted to fly into his arms. He came in on crutches and his body was all patched up, but it was Michael!

"Hi Sweetie," he said softly smiling with his eyes. "How's my girl?"

Tears streaming down my face I said, "All better now."

CHAPTER 19

House Guest

I got to go home in a couple of days, as promised and Michael came back after a week. He was in Boston to have plastic surgery on his face to repair all the damage from the accident. He would have a long recovery once at home.

Alcott brought Michael home from Boston and, as ordered by Maggie brought him straight to our house. He was happy Alcott was bringing him to see me, but he didn't know he wouldn't be bringing him home afterwards. He was surprised to see his parents, Ken and Ida there.

"I've set up a room for you upstairs, Michael," began Maggie. "I'll not have you going off on your own as yet. And don't even try to argue with me, you hear?"

"Yes, ma'am, I mean no, ma'am. I wouldn't dream of arguing with you, Maggie."

Everyone laughed and Maggie set off to make some tea.

"I will have to get back to work soon though," Michael tried.

"You'll do nothing of the sort, Michael Curtis Brennan," said his mother with authority! "You need to take care of that leg of yours before you go taking care of the world. Have you forgotten about the crutches you are on? How do you think you're going to work while holding crutches? You're a doctor. You know better."

"Ok, Mom, I'll give it a week," said Michael, "and then I'm going back to work, crutches or no crutches. I've been on these things long enough anyway."

"Has he always been this stubborn, Ida," I asked?

"Yes he has."

"I'm going to go help Maggie with the tea," I said.

"No you won't," called Maggie from the kitchen. "I promised the doctor you wouldn't lift a finger if he let me bring you home. You sit right back down. Since when can't I make a pot of tea on my own anyway?"

We had our tea and Ida, Ken and Alcott decided it was time for them to leave. Everyone was tired and it had been a long day.

Ida felt bad that she couldn't care for Michael herself, but she and Ken both had full time jobs and Michael couldn't be alone right now. "I'm so grateful to you, Maggie for taking in our son. I'll be by each night to spell you for awhile."

"Oh, it's no problem. I enjoy caring for him and he'll be good company for Sharon. Don't give it a second thought."

And with that, the house was empty except me, Maggie and Michael.

CHAPTER 20

Sprung!

The week passed quickly. I was so enjoying having Michael stay with us and I was feeling so much better. I wasn't too happy about the tuft of hair that was starting to stick up on top of my head where they did the surgery, but it sure beat the alternative. I was no longer on house arrest and had been helping out with Michael for the past two days. He and I spent time sitting under the willow tree, being sure to stay in the shade. And on rainy days, we stayed inside and played backgammon over and over again.

Michael was rapidly on the mend and the surgeon had done such an amazing job, that I was beginning to see my Michael again. None of us really knew what the outcome of the surgery would be, but it was incredible. He was healing so well that you could barely see where he was stitched.

"Sharon," Michael said, "I'm having a wonderful time being with you, but I do have to go home. "What do you say we go out and have breakfast at the Black Dog? Since I've graduated to the cane, it's a lot easier for me to get around."

Then to Maggie. "Nothing against your cooking Maggie, it's some of the best I've ever had and I will truly miss it when I have to fend for myself again, but I just want to treat you girls to a meal out. What do you say?"

"I'm in," I said.

"Okay then. I guess I'm in too," Maggie said.

Then, from around the back of the house and through the open window, "I'm in," came Thomas' voice.

We all laughed because that man could hear a flea sneeze unless you wanted him to hear the flea sneeze.

We all pigged out at breakfast. The sea air really makes people hungry, I swear. We shared a large order of my favorite, Black Dog's famous home fries with bacon and broccoli and smothered in cheese. As if that wasn't enough we had huge omelets. Mine had ham and cheese and came with homemade raisin toast. We stuffed ourselves blind and headed home.

Maggie wanted to get back and do some house cleaning and Thomas wanted to tend the garden, so we brought them home and headed back out. Just the two of us. I had to drive because Michael wasn't cleared to yet, so I started back from where we came towards one of my favorite shops on the island. "Bowl and Board" had great things to look at and I loved puttering around there. I could use a new wooden salad bowl.

After that we went to the kitchen store where I always picked up a new chocolate from somewhere in the world with unique flavors. This time I got pink peppercorn dark chocolate from Spain. When I bit into it, wonderful crunchy bites of pepper invaded my mouth. It was incredible.

I loved all the salts they imported too. This time, to keep the theme going, I got pink sea salt. The crystals were large and I couldn't wait to sprinkle them on my chocolate dipped caramels I would make for the next special occasion.

I could tell Michael was getting tired of walking, so we headed back to the car and home for awhile. He wanted to attend "Illumination" tonight but I told him we would drive there and just sit in our car and watch. He agreed to my terms.

That evening we drove along the waterfront. It was a hot night in August, with a cool breeze coming off the ocean as we got out of the car and found a free bench to sit on. We were just a few minutes away from Grand Illumination in Oak Bluffs.

The streets are lined with people waiting for the moment when the lights are lit. Each cottage is adorned beautifully with colorful Chinese and Japanese lanterns and both, the band and Community Sing stand ready to play in the Tabernacle. It truly is a magical sight.

Michael was holding my hand when he turned toward me and said, "Sharon, I love you so much. I'd get down on my knee to say this, but unfortunately my knee is not quite bendable yet." He smiled and continued, "I've waited a lifetime to ask you this question and now that the time is here, I'm not sure what to say, except, Sharon, will you marry me?" He fumbled in his pocket and pulled out a beautiful solitaire diamond ring and put it on my finger.

I was so happy; I grabbed him and hugged him and answered, "What took you so long?" We both just laughed, and in that perfect moment, the town was illuminated and so was I.

Later, when we were riding along Shore Road, Michael said, "I can't wait to tell my parents, do you mind if we stop by? I mentioned to them that I was going to ask you tonight, even though I hadn't had time to go shopping for a ring. They were so happy that my mom went into her bedroom and came back out with her mother's diamond ring. The very ring you now wear, sweetie."

I looked down at my ring. "Oh, Michael, this was your grandmother's? That makes it even more precious. Yes, let's go to your parents. I really need to thank them for so much, and now for this beautiful gift."

We arrived a few minutes later and were greeted on the front porch by Ida and Ken. They must've been waiting for Michael to come home with his report. They rushed outside to hear the news. They stopped short and regained their composure, then, playing it cool, Ida said, "Well, what a nice surprise to see you two tonight. What brings you here?"

"Hi, Mom," started Michael. "I already told Sharon that you knew what I was up to tonight, so you can cut the coy act. Good try though." He laughed as he gave his mother a kiss on the cheek.

"Oh, I'm so happy for you two," Ida said.

"Give them some room to come in dear," Ken said from behind his wife. "Congratulations. We couldn't be happier." Ken hugged me and then Michael and we all went inside. Seated and toasting with champagne, already on ice, Ken added, "If I could've handpicked a wife for Michael, Sharon, you would have been my choice as well. You're the daughter that Ida and I never had."

"Thank you so much. Both of you, for everything," I began. "I mean, I don't know how I would've dealt with all the happenings the last couple of months without your support. I know Michael and I are going to be very happy together. And I couldn't have asked for better in-laws than you."

"Now that you're going to be our new daughter, you can stop calling us Ken and Ida. We'd love it if you'd call us Mom and Dad," offered Ida.

A tear came to my eye. I hadn't called anyone Mom or Dad except my own and I didn't know if I was ready to call someone else that yet. I really missed having my parents around. I was overwhelmed by the gesture though and managed, "Thank you...Mom....Dad."

We made our way to the screened in porch on the back of the house that overlooked the magnificent harbor view in Edgartown.

"So," asked Ken, "when is the big day?"

Michael and I looked at each other and kind of shrugged our shoulders and smiled. "Well, I don't know, Michael, what do you think? I mean we really haven't had time to think about that yet."

"Yeah, I was just hoping to get a 'yes'. I didn't think past that," said Michael. "But I do have a date that sticks in my head. Sharon, do you remember when we were kids and I hung around your brother all the time?"

"Of course. You were at my house all the time. How could I forget; you were so annoying," I played.

"Well, there was one day in particular that I relive in my dreams all the time."

"You dream about me, Michael," I asked?

"I've always dreamed about you, Sharon. There's never been anyone else for me and there never will be again," said Michael sincerely. There was a day when we were all playing around your house and we were about ten years old. We decided to play house and I was the father and you were the mother. Do you remember this?"

"We played that game a lot, it seems now that I think about it. You were always trying to kiss me and I was always running away from you," I said, laughing at the memory.

"That's right, but this time I had decided that if we were going to play house, we needed to get married. I had taken my dad's bow tie that day before I went over your house and a lace tablecloth from the linen drawer..."

"Michael David Brennan," exclaimed Ida! That was my mother's!"

"Yeah," Ken chimed in, "I wondered where that tie went."

"Sorry Mom, Dad, anyway ..."

"I remember," interrupted Sharon! "I wore that lace table cloth on my head for a veil and wrapped it around my body for the dress. I thought I looked so beautiful in that table cloth."

"You did, Sharon," continued Michael. "Well, that day we were married in your parents' gazebo overlooking the ocean. It was just fun to you, but to me, it was the greatest moment in my life, up until you agreed to marry me for real, of course. I remember that day we were playing because it was the last day of school vacation. The date was September 2nd. That's the perfect date for our wedding. What do you think, Sharon?"

"I think the fact that you remembered that date is very

romantic, sweet and yes, a little disturbing,"" I laughed. "And I definitely want to marry you on September 2nd, Michael! I would love to recreate that moment in my parents' gazebo at home. The weather will still be glorious, but..." I looked down unable to finish my sentence.

"But what," asked Michael concerned?

"My brother was the best man that day, and my parents are gone."

"I'm sorry, Sharon," said Michael feeling my pain. "I miss them too. Very much! Shon was my best friend. Wait here."

Michael ran inside then came back out with an old shoebox and handed it to me. "Open it!"

I opened the box and inside it was his mother's lace tablecloth. His mother and I just wept as I pulled it out of the box. Underneath it was his father's tie.

Later that night Michael took me home so we could tell Maggie. When we got there the whole house smelled like bread. How I love the smell of freshly baked bread. We went into the kitchen and scoffed a couple of slices, slathered them in butter and shoved them in our mouths as if we hadn't eaten in weeks.

I reached for another piece when Maggie slapped my hand away and told me to sit down. "I'll make you a proper meal. Don't you go filling up on bread. Sit down, Michael dear and I'll be with you both in a moment."

However, I had Maggie wrapped around my little finger since I can remember, so I shot her my best pout and she handed me another piece of bread. She also put out some thick slices of ham and brought out some freshly made iced tea with peaches.

"We have some news for you Maggie," Michael managed between bites.

"Well, what is it," asked Maggie impatiently? "Out with it, child!"

I managed to stop eating long enough to cut in, "Michael asked me to marry him Maggie!"

Maggie jumped up from the table and hugged and kissed us both. "This is so wonderful! Oh, I can't wait to hear the pitter patter of little feet in this 'ole house again."

"Whoah," I said, "Slow down, Mags. Little feet? Whose little feet? We're not even married yet and you've got me barefoot and pregnant."

Brandy, Maggie's overzealous dog was jumping up and down and barking from all the excitement. We were all having a good laugh. I sat back and enjoyed the rest of my meal in complete and utter bliss at the thought of having a family again.

CHAPTER 21

My Wedding Day

It's been a glorious summer. A summer filled with long walks on the beach and wedding plans. I came to terms with my past while planning my future.

Today is September 2nd and, as planned it is also my wedding day. It's a gorgeous sunny, warm day. The tents are up, the tables set and the flowers in their places. The gazebo is decorated with purple wisteria and red roses. It's the most beautiful setting for a wedding. All of the flowers came from the garden that Thomas has been working so hard on all these years.

Thomas has carefully transplanted every kind of flower available into pots, so they could be put back into the garden after the ceremony. My friend, Cynthia makes the most beautiful clay pots in her studio and gave us a dozen of them as a wedding gift when we tried to buy them. What a treasure they are to us.

I just love our lilac trees for their amazing fragrance and the daisies for their simplicity. Everything came together easily thanks to our friends and family.

Maggie made the wedding cake, complete with a fountain filled with pink lemonade (my favorite). It is spectacular!

Alcott, who is practically part of the family now and is in a band, volunteered to play at our wedding. He plays a mix of blues and soft rock that we can't get enough of.

Thomas, being the closest thing I have to a father figure now agreed to give me away. I think I saw a tear form in his kind eyes when I asked him. I am so grateful to have him, yet sad that Dad, Mom and Shon are not here for the greatest day of my life.

Maggie was helping me get ready and as I was getting into my gown she said, "Sharon, darlin', I have something old for you to wear today. I've been saving it for you." She looked melancholy as she went to her jewelry box and pulled out a cameo.

"Mom's brooch," I cried! "Where did you ever find it Maggie?"

"'Twas left to me in your mum's will, Sharon dear, with a note." And with that she handed me a small, pink envelope that smelled of lavender; mom's favorite scent. It was addressed to Maggie and it was in her own handwriting. I could just see her hand holding the pen and writing this note. I miss her gentle hands.

My Dearest Maggie,

You have been with our family for many years and if you are reading this note, my husband and I are both gone from this world. I leave you in charge of my most precious possessions; my daughter Sharon and my great-great grandmother's cameo. My wish is for you to give the cameo to Sharon on her wedding day, as it has been a tradition for the eldest daughter in the family to receive this heirloom on this special day for generations. Please give her the other note in the box.

Your devoted friend in Christ,

Elizabeth

I couldn't contain my tears as Maggie pinned the brooch on my wedding gown then handed me the other letter. "It's for your eyes only, Sharon. I'll give you a few minutes. I'll just be down in the kitchen looking things over."

I nodded and looked down at the envelope, also in pink and also smelling of lavender perfume. I ran my hands gently over it and held it up to my face, knowing my mother had touched it. Then I slowly and carefully opened it.

My Dear Sweet Sharon,

Oh, sweetie, how I wish I were there with you now. I'm sure you're the most beautiful bride there ever was. I'm watching you now and whomever you have chosen to spend your life with I'm sure I love him too. My wedding dress, if you chose to wear it, I'm sure is stunning and every head will turn when they see you in it.

The brooch compliments the dress beautifully. Each of us from your great-great grandmother to me and now you has worn this brooch on their wedding day. Please carry on the tradition with your own children. Your father and I love you very much. Congratulations! Know, today, that Dad and I are looking down on you and smiling and that we will be dancing at your wedding.

Loving you always,

Mom

Outside the guests were being ushered to their seats as I tried to collect myself and reapply the makeup I had just washed away with my tears. I was happy to be marrying Michael and I was happy to have a piece of my Mom with me too. I could hear the music start to play and headed downstairs.

Alcott's three year old daughter, Ellie was the flower girl and she was adorable in her white dress draped in daisies and a wreath of the same adorning her beautiful head of thick, brown curly ringlets. Her mother had died in childbirth, which left Alcott to raise her alone. Now he has been able to start over on this Island where he has become so well known and loved. Maggie watched Ellie during the day when Alcott was working, so I had been able to get to know her pretty well.

Next, the two junior bridesmaids walked down the aisle of tiny white pebbles leading to the gazebo where the crowd was assembled. Cecily and Caron were the eight year old twins of Ida and Ken's long time friends and neighbors, the Jordan's. The girls wore lilac gowns that were trimmed in iridescent pearls and they carried bouquets of purple lilacs and green ivy from our garden.

The wedding march began to play and everyone stood and turned towards me. It was intimidating to say the least. I never liked being the center of attention. There I stood, Sharon Rose Walsh, soon to be Mrs. Michael Brennan, MD. I felt beautiful in my mother's wedding gown of satin and lace and somehow felt her arms wrapped around me as I wore it. My bouquet was a thing of beauty that Thomas put together for me. It was filled with lilacs, daisies, roses of every hue, ivy and a mixture of colors and textures that completed the display. I always loved a lot of color.

The sea breeze was gently whispering in my ear as the music played sweetly in the background. Up ahead of me, standing next to Pastor Bob, was my future. This was the moment that I would leave the past behind and walk straight into Michael's arms, where I would be safe forever.

Thomas lent his arm to me and whispered, "Sharon dear, you're a beautiful bride and I wish you all the best with Michael. He is a good man and he loves you very much, and so do I. Are you ready?"

He had never said that to me before and my heart swelled with joy and love.

I looked down the aisle at my Michael who was smiling at me and looking devastatingly handsome in his white tails and lavender cumber bun and handkerchief. I turned, gave Thomas a kiss on the cheek and said, "I'm ready. Let's do this."

As I approached the gazebo Michael reached out a hand and led me up the steps. He was beaming with pride when he looked into my eyes. This was his day; the day he had hoped for since we were children. I'm so blessed to be able to make a man like this happy.

Pastor Bob began, "Do you Michael, take Sharon to be your lawfully wedded wife? Do you promise before God and all of your friends and family to be good to her and cherish your every moment with her?"

"I do," came the obvious answer from the man who could not; would not take his eyes off of me.

"Sharon, do you take Michael to be your lawfully wedded husband? Do you promise before God and all of your friends and family to be good to him and cherish your every moment with him?"

"I do."

"Now, Michael and Sharon, you may exchange your own vows which you have written."

I looked at Michael and said, "Michael, I love you with all my heart and I promise to be true to you always. I will love you in good times and in bad. Whether we have enough money or struggling to survive. I will be by your side forever until we are parted by death. Michael you are my best friend. I place this ring on your finger as a token of my endless love. This is my vow to you."

When he took my hand in his I wished we were alone because standing there in front of everyone was so difficult. I hate to cry in front of people and it seemed it was all I was doing. Then he spoke and took all the pressure off of me.

"Sharon, darling, you are my breath and my life. I promise that I will care for you forever and never be untrue. I am so happy that you have agreed to be my wife. I have loved you since we were kids and never dreamed this day would actually come. Well, I dreamed it, but I didn't really believe dreams could come true until this very moment. You are so much more to me than a wife and a friend. You are my soul. I love you so much, my dear, sweet Sharon Rose and I want you to know that I am here for you, always. I place this ring on your finger as a token of my endless love. This is my vow to you."

"I now proclaim that here and now in the face of all who view and in the eyes of our Almighty God and Savior, that Michael and Sharon are husband and wife! You may kiss the bride."

Everyone stood up and cheered, but I heard nothing as Michael kissed me. It was a surreal moment and I was swept away by the moment. Finally, we turned to face the crowd and, hand in hand walked down the stairs as Mr. & Mrs. Brennan.

CHAPTER 22

The Reception

The bridesmaids were in silver slip dresses made of silk that flowed to the knee while the maid of honor, my friend Brielle, who came from Boston, was in lavender taffeta with Swarovski crystals exploding all over the fabric. Her spaghetti straps were also lined in crystals and she wore a small crown atop her beautifully quaffed hair. The ushers were in sleek, black tuxedos with shirts to match their bridesmaid partners and a bold stripe down the sides of their pants in the same color.

Alcott did the announcing as each couple entered the garden and when it came to introducing Michael and I, everyone got on their feet and started clapping and whistling. I could barely hear his announcement through all the hoopla. We just laughed.

A few minutes later, Michael's Best Man and long time friend, David Fletcher, Fletch as we called him, original, I know, gave the toast.

"I'd like to make a toast to Sharon and Michael," he began. "Sharon, I've had to listen to Michael ooze over you for the past twenty plus years. He has always loved you. My wish for you is that now that you've found each other again, that you are always kind, loving and respectful to one another. And so, Michael and Sharon, I say this to you:

Never let the sun set in anger...

Always work it out,

And cherish your love like there is no other love in the world."

With that said David raised his glass to us and we all drank our sparkling apple juice. I did not want any alcohol at the wedding since I decided to give up drinking and start living my life as God intended.

I had gone off the deep end after my brother died and it came to a point where I needed to wake up and get on with my life. I almost died a couple of times because of my partying; I think I may have wanted to join my brother for awhile there and didn't really care about living. I'm so glad I felt that God was trying to tell me I had a future and that I listened.

The reception went on and the food was served. We had lobster, courtesy of David's commercial business, and prime rib with steamed clams that Michael, David, Alcott and Thomas dug tirelessly all week, red potatoes, corn on the cob and kielbasa. This was all on a buffet so everyone could have their fill. I had two lobsters, about a pound of clams, some kielbasa and a piece of corn. Then came dessert provided by Kathie's Kitchen, who also made killer appetizers for us. As if we didn't have enough, Kathie threw in a couple dozen loaves of assorted homemade breads.

About an hour into the reception a waiter came over to my table and asked if I needed anything. I looked up at him to reply and felt the blood leave my face. I thought I would pass out.

"Ma'am," he said. "Are you okay? You look like you've just seen a ghost."

I managed to stand up, wobbly as I was, look at him and just before my world went black I managed, "Shon?"

CHAPTER 23

What Did She Just Say?

I opened my eyes to find that I was on the ground, surrounded by a crowd of people. "Are you okay, Sharon," Michael asked me? "You fainted."

Am I okay? I don't know. Why am I on the ground? Why is everyone looking at me? Suddenly I remembered! Shon! I jumped up as fast as I could and shoved the crowed aside as I searched the room. Maggie spoke, "Sharon, dear, I heard you called a waiter Shon. Shon is dead sweetie. Remember?"

I snapped at her, my beloved Maggie, "Of course I remember! It's all I think about! But I'm telling you, the man that just came to my table is Shon!!"

Everyone must've thought I was having a break down. I could hear them all murmuring.

"Ok, Sharon," said Michael, "someone went to get the waiter. When he comes back we'll straighten all this out. Let's sit down for a minute, you're still a bit weak. Have some water, please."

Just then David came up behind Michael and started whispering. I could barely hear him, but it sounded like he was saying the waiter was by the buffet table and he, indeed looked like Shon!

Michael and I looked over in that direction as the man came towards us again. I heard Michael almost scream as he saw what I had seen just minutes ago. My dead brother was at our wedding.

"How can this be," Michael said to Shon as he arrived. "They found your body."

I had dreamed of this moment so many times. I knew I would wake up from this dream any minute now, then he spoke. "You wanted to see me, ma'am?"

He didn't know me. Shon didn't know me. What's wrong with you, I wanted to shout! Where have you been?! How did you get here now?!

I could hear Maggie talking to others saying, "And, don't you know how much Sharon misses her Mum and Dad as well as her dear, sweet brother, Shon, Lord rest their souls. She's just distraught is all."

Shon turned around, "I know that voice. I know that woman from somewhere," he said as he saw Maggie. "Who is she?"

"That's Maggie," I said gently, realizing that Shon did not know who he was. "She's our housekeeper and practically family. Do you know me, Shon?"

"Why did you call me Shon? Why is everyone calling me Shon? Has everyone gone crazy in this heat or what? I need to go talk to that woman, Maggie is it?"

As Shon and I approached Maggie she jumped out of her chair and with as much grace as a bull in a china shop ran over to Shon, throwing her arms around him and hugged him with the strength of a superhero. "Praise God!! Is it really you?! Shon, me darling?!" She noticed his searching expression and calmed herself. "Don't you know me, Shon, darlin'? Where have you been all these years?"

Once Maggie released her death grip, Shon said to her, "Ma'am, why do you call me by the name of Shon? You're the third person to do that today. You seem so familiar to me, yet I'm sure I can't figure out where we've met before."

Maggie looked up at me with determined strength, letting me know I was not alone in this as she took Shon's hands in hers. "I call you Shon, dear, because that's your given name. You've come home to us, you have. Don't you know, Shon that you had a boat accident many years ago? We were told you were dead. But you're here, standing right in front of my eyes, you are."

He looked back at the house and looked up to the second floor. He was looking at his old bedroom window that overlooked the ocean. He looked back at Maggie and said, "That window. I know it. Did I stay there? Why did I stay there? Who did I come here with?"

Maggie happily answered, "Aye, 'tis your bedroom window, Shon. This is your childhood home, don't you know. We've left it as it was before you.... As it always was. Come, see if you know it." At that, Maggie, Shon and I went into the house.

Shon mentioned the familiar smell of baked bread and apples as we approached the front door. "When I was younger someone used to bake bread for me and it made the house smell as wonderful as this does now."

"That was me, darlin'," offered Maggie. "I baked fresh bread for you and your family every Sunday morning."

I finally was ready and I touched Shon on the shoulder. "Can it be? It is, I know it is, but I don't believe it or understand it. Shon. You are my brother, Shon." I hugged him as I fell into a puddle of tears; tears of joy and years of pain.

"Again with Shon. I don't understand. Look, I'd really like to be your brother, Mrs. Brennan, you seem nice enough, but I don't understand what all this is about. I'm just a caterer, at a wedding. I'm sorry."

"Ten years ago," I began, boldly, "you went out in your boat and never came back. That is, until today. The police came to the house and told us you were dead and they couldn't find your body, but after awhile they did find your body, or someone's body. I don't know how, but you are standing right in front of me and you are my brother Shon!"

"Wait a minute," said Shon. "I did have a boating accident that long ago, but no one ever called me Shon before. The people that helped me told me that I was floating near a sandbar off of Nantucket when they happened along and fished me out of the water. They didn't know how I got there, but assumed I lived on Nantucket. I've lived there as long as I can remember back. I assumed

I had no family and that's why I knew no one on the Island. I've been married to Kathie for five years now and we started this catering business about two years ago. We have a little girl named Sharon. I always liked that name, Sharon."

Tears still flowing I said to him, "I'm Sharon."

CHAPTER 24

The Awakening

Shon seemed to suddenly snap out of his ten year trance. "Sharon! My sister, Sharon!!" He grabbed me so hard I could barely breathe and we sobbed in each other's arms for a good long time. When we finally let go he said, "I remember! I remember it all! Maggie!" He hugged her, then, "How I've missed you both, I just didn't know it was you I missed. I've had such a hole in my heart, a longing... I'm home! I'm home!"

Just then Michael walked in, hearing all the commotion. "Michael!" Shon was so happy to see his best friend. Michael was shocked and excited all at once. They did their ridiculous man dance they had concocted since childhood and we all laughed. Happy again.

"No more work for you today, Shon," I said. "You are going to dance with me!" And with that, I swept him away.

After a few dances, Shon's wife came up to us and said, "What do you think you're doing?"

"I'm dancing with my sister," he said and swept me away. I could see the shocked look on Kathie's face, but we had lots of time to fill her in.

Towards the end of the wedding and lots of dances with Michael and Shon and Maggie, I sat down and Shon came over and asked, "Hey, where are Mum and Dad? I've been so distracted, that I haven't even seen them yet. I can't wait to see them."

I looked at him and had to tell him that they were gone. He just got his family back only to find out that half of them were no longer living.

After all the guests left, Shon and Kathie packed up their van to catch the last ferry back to Nantucket. We hugged goodbye, but I did not want to let him out of my sight. "You know Sharon," he said, "if we didn't already commit to that catering job in Nantucket in a few days, we wouldn't leave tonight. It's a miracle that this day even happened. I mean I've been Patrick Harris for ten years and now I find out that I'm Shon Walsh and have a sister. I'll have to legally change our whole family's names. Maybe we can have a celebration here."

"This is our home, Shon. Of course we can do anything you like. But you guys cannot cater it, we will have a backyard bar-b-que and just be real laid back. I think we've had enough excitement for awhile."

In the back of my mind I was terrified to say goodbye,

remembering the last time I did that with Shon.

Maggie came running out of the house like she was on fire, "Wait up! I made you some bread." She put it in his hands and looked into his eyes for a moment, "now be off with you or you'll miss your ... boat."

"We'll be back next Saturday, you silly old woman," he teased as he always had in the past.

I hugged him goodbye, then his wife, Kathie as she said to me, "I always wanted a sister."

CHAPTER 25

The Honeymoon

Michael and I drove down to Edgartown to the Harbor Inn for our wedding night. It was a beautiful evening and we were still on a high from the wedding and finding Shon. The stars carpeted the sky, surrounding the almost full moon, which lit our little piece of earth abundantly as it kissed the ocean, leaving a sparkling trail.

I love how Michael always opens my car door and I felt elated as he took my hand and we looked into each other's eyes. I know he could see the happiness I hadn't felt in too many years. He took my face in his hands and kissed me gently on the lips. "Darling, you are more beautiful than all the princesses that have ever been created, and I promise to try to give you a happily ever after. Now kiss me like you mean it."

Once in the room I allowed myself total abandon with Michael for the very first time. No more holding back. I kissed him with the passion of a thousand arrows from Cupid's bow. It was wonderful and it felt right. I truly love making love to this man.

While we were lying there in each other's arms, we heard a knock on the door. "Room service." I didn't order room service and Michael didn't order room service. Michael went to the door.

The man rolled in a cart with chilled sparkling cider, shrimp cocktail, fresh strawberries and cream and crackers and cheese. "Compliments of Alcott Smallcombe," announced the waiter as he nodded and left the room.

"How sweet," I said. It was sweet. He had become a good friend to us all. We were ravenous and it was perfect timing.

"The last thing I need is Alcott on my bride's mind right now, with his perfectly chiseled body," Michael said out of nowhere.

"What are you talking about," I asked?

"I can't believe he would intrude on our honeymoon like this."

"He sent a gift, Michael, that's all. I'm not thinking about anyone but you. I married you and I love you. Really? Are you really upset about this gift? I'm starving; I see it as food and that's it. You want some?" I held a strawberry up to his mouth then teasingly, took it back and bit it sensually.

"Come to think of it, I am hungry," he said with a sexy smirk.

CHAPTER 26

The Morning After

"Good morning, Mrs. Brennan," Michael said leaning over the bed to kiss me.

"Good morning to you, Mr. Brennan," I replied in my happy, sleepy state.

"How amazing is it that not only did I get to marry you," Michael began, "but that Shon was there?! I'm still flying high about it all and I'm so glad that our children will know their Uncle Shon."

He was so excited by this delivery I almost laughed, but... "Whoah! Back up a minute," I said. "Children? Who said anything about children?"

"Well, we may just have made our first last night Poo-Poo-Face," he laughed.

"Poo-Poo-Face? That's to be my pet name? Okay, fair is fair, Cucca-Head."

"Oh, come on, you can do better than that, can't you?"

"Give me some time, I'll work on it. Now come over here and kiss me," I said. "This isn't over."

"I'm so hungry right now."

Michael touched my stomach and said, "And what does my baby want for breakfast?"

Playing along, I answered, "I don't know about little Crystal Rose, but I want pancakes and a rash of bacon with lots of butter and syrup, STAT!"

"Crystal Rose, is it? Well, are you sure that's all you want, because I know a few people and I'm sure I can get a whole pig delivered if that's what my princess wants."

"Come to think of it," I said, "I do want some sausages too. Oh yeah, and a great big glass of ice cold chocolate milk."

"I'm glad I asked," Michael added. "I'll have room service haul it right up."

Michael got himself a tropical fruit cup with cantaloupe, mango and pineapple along with a bowl of cornflakes and a cup of coffee. I ate my breakfast as if it was my last and when I looked up for a breath, Michael was watching in horror.

"How do you feel about taking out the 'Mary Elizabeth' today," Michael asked. "We can sail over to Cape Poge for awhile. We'll bring a picnic lunch and just bake all day in the sun. It's a gorgeous day and it's the one place we can be completely alone. I know I'm selfish, but I want you all to myself today."

"That sounds good to me, Michael. It's a perfect day to go sailing. Let me take a quick bath and we can get going. What do you want to pack for lunch?"

"I'll have the restaurant downstairs throw something special together for us. I'm sure they'll know what to do," Michael said.

"We can grab towels and a throw at home before we leave," I added.

No one was at home when we got there, which was strange. "Maggie must've gone out with Thomas in the Whaler," I said. "I'll run up and get the towels and blanket. Be right back."

When I came back downstairs, Michael was holding a picnic basket and a note.

"Where did that come from," I asked?

"Maggie left it. Here's the note."

My Dearest Sharon and Michael,

I knew you'd be wanting to go out on the water today so I made you some goodies. There's a basket in the fridge. Enjoy!

Love, Maggie

We looked in the basket and it had Maggie's famous fried chicken, potato salad and fresh crusty bread. "We'll have a feast with all the fruit and calzones the restaurant packed for us and now this, we can stay out to sea for a week," Michael said.

We loaded up the boat and set sail. There was a gentle breeze which took us where we wanted to go. The sky was blue everywhere we looked and the ocean calm. The temperature outside was just hot enough to merit a swim. As we approached our destination where the water looks like glass, Michael dropped anchor. I couldn't wait, so I jumped right in and swam for it. I wasn't much help carrying the goodies, but Michael didn't seem to mind. He put everything on a big foam board we use for floating on the water and just guided it to the shore.

We spent a wonderfully relaxing day alone and all my stress was lifted. We had blueberry iced tea with berries in it as we sat in the warm spring on the other side of the sand. "It just doesn't get any better than this," said Michael with his arm around me.

We ate a good amount of the food throughout the day and swam. We even tied our floating foam to the boat and floated for awhile. The water gently began rocking me to sleep, but Michael woke me. "We should be heading out soon, Sharon, the wind is perfect right now to take us home."

I looked up and realized he was just trying not to scare me because I saw how the sky had become dark all of a sudden. We hadn't been expecting a storm, but you never knew out in the ocean what would happen. Just to be safe we decided to head home as the clouds were rolling in.

We had just gotten everything back on the boat and Michael was helping me in when it started raining. A little at first and then suddenly wildly. Michael jumped into the boat and started the engine. He wasn't taking a chance on tipping over with the sails up. He told me to go below so I could keep dry and safe as he began pulling the sails.

We were heading home and the waves were getting very high. I was afraid, but trusted my Michael completely. The boat started rocking and the waves were coming up over the bow. Lightening struck the mast and caught it on fire. I went to the surface to see what had happened and grabbed the fire extinguisher to put it out.

Michael was telling me to get below and trying to control the boat that was now uncontrollably being tossed about by the sea like a tub toy. I decided that I was just in the way and I went below to do the only thing I knew could help. I prayed. "Dear Jesus, please help get us safely back home. Keep my husband safe, Lord and show him the way. I just got my life back together and I'm sorry for all the time I lost. Forgive me, please! Save us, Lord. Save us!"

In that moment I wondered if my brother had even had time to pray before his boat went down. I won't think about all that right now. I refuse to give in to fear. This is not going to happen to us! We'll be fine. We're perfectly safe. Michael is an accomplished sailor and I'm the best first mate he could have. I tried to convince myself but all I could think was, Shon was a great boater too.

The storm stopped as suddenly as it had started and we were almost home. It was going to be alright. "Thank you Jesus. Thank you for everything."

As we pulled into dock, Maggie came running. She was frantic. "Oh, Sharon! Michael! We were so worried about you, Thomas and I. As soon as the storm came in, we tied up the whaler and realized the sailboat was out. We held hands and prayed 'til we saw you come around the corner. The Lord brought you back to me."

"We're fine Maggie," said Michael, "just a little shaken up is all. We could use some warm tea and dry clothes. Let's head in."

We all sat around the fire, Michael, Maggie, Thomas and I and talked about how we came through the storm and about the wedding day. We talked well into the night. I actually fell asleep on the plush rug in front of the fireplace. The sounds of family talking quietly lulled me to sleep, just as they always had.

CHAPTER 27

Alcott's Visit

The following morning, since everyone slept in late, it was about noontime when I got up. Someone was at the front door and I didn't want to wake up Michael, so I slipped away quietly to answer it. Alcott had been patrolling the docks when he looked over and saw the 'Mary Elizabeth' with a broken mast. "I came to see if you were alright," he said. "I saw the boat. What happened? Don't tell me you were out in that storm yesterday."

"Come on in Alcott," I said between yawns. "I'll tell you all about it. But first, coffee."

So, while the house slept, we sat in the kitchen talking about yesterday's adventure. We talked about Shon and ate whatever food I could scrounge up. We had pretty much cleaned out the pantry the night before.

Maggie came in and saw us eating cold chicken for breakfast and went to town trying to find something, anything better than that to put in our bellies. "Well, good morning to you darlin'," she said to me and, "welcome Alcott," to our guest. "What brings you out here on a work day?"

"I was just telling Sharon that I saw the boat's broken mast and was concerned. She already filled me in. I'm real glad everyone's alright. You've all become pretty much family to me here on the island."

"Well, you're family to us too, Alcott," said Maggie. "And I won't have you eating cold chicken for breakfast. Now you two sit there while I make you something hot."

Thomas and Michael woke up and came into the kitchen to join the group. "Good morning all," came Michael's greeting. "Hey Alcott, good to see you."

"Good to see you too, Michael; I heard about your wild boat ride yesterday."

"Yeah, it was a little hairy for awhile there," said Michael, "but thanks to Sharon's quick thinking, she got the fire out and I was able to steer us in."

"You make a great team," said Thomas. "I knew you would," he said with a wink.

"Thank you, Thomas," I said, kissing his cheek. "You're so sweet. So," I continued, smiling mischievously at Maggie, "when are you two getting married?"

"Sharon Rose Walsh," Maggie yelled through her embarrassment!

"It's Brennan now," I teased back.

"You know what I mean!"

"That is a very good question," added Thomas. "When are you going to marry me woman?"

They all looked at Maggie waiting for her response, expecting it to be a wild denial, when she called his bluff. "How about tomorrow," was all she said with a smart allecy attitude?

"Tomorrow?! What," stumbled Thomas. "Are you serious or are you playing games with me? I'm too old for games Margaret Rose Mulcahey!"

"Well, if it will shut you all up once and for all, let's do it tomorrow. Alcott, you're a Justice of the Peace aren't you," she asked?

"I'm actually an ordained Minister."

"Even better," said Maggie! "Will you marry us tomorrow? Right here in this house?"

Jaws were dropping faster than the pancakes she was flipping. "I'd be honored, Maggie," said Alcott, "that is if the groom is willing."

"Well, that's done, now all of you get going! I have things to be doing. Take the pancakes with you."

And then it was settled. Thomas didn't need to reply. It was what he always wanted. Not exactly the way he heard her answer in his head, but it would do. We all scattered to put a quick wedding together. I called Shon and invited him and his family over, then I called some of Maggie and Thomas' friends.

Maggie was getting her wish; the house would be full now. Maggie, Thomas, Michael and I would share this large and for some time, too empty home. We would now be family like we always should have been.

CHAPTER 28

Maggie & Thomas

Michael and I woke up to another beautiful day on the island. The sun was streaming through our bedroom window, lighting the room in all its magnificence as the seagulls sang their morning song to us.

I stretched my arms above my head and yawned. Michael put his arm around me and said, "Good morning, darling. You look well rested. There's a lot of commotion going on downstairs. It sounds like everyone else is already setting up the chairs and tables. Thank God Shon and Kathie offered to bring the food. They must've been up all night cooking. We better get down there and help."

I brought my hands down around Michael's neck and hugged him. "Michael, I can't tell you how happy I am right now. What could be more perfect? We are married, Shon is alive and Maggie is finally marrying Thomas. I just wish my Mom and Dad could see this day."

"Yeah, me too, Sharon. Me too. I wish I could make that happen for you."

"Oh, you have made my world so much less lonely, Michael. It's just times like these that I really think about them. I love you so much, sweetie and that's all I need right now. Just your love."

I was walking by Maggie's bedroom on my way downstairs when I saw her standing in the window, looking out. I could see the side of her face and she seemed truly happy. As I was about to walk away, I heard her speak to the air, "Well, Mary, James, I'm finally going to marry Thomas."

She was talking to my parents. I stayed and listened. "Mary dear, you encouraged me to do this so many years ago when you were here and I didn't because I wanted to care for you and the kids and stay here with you. Then you both died and I stayed by myself to be sure the place stayed nice for our Sharon. I just knew she would come back one day and I didn't want her to come home to an empty house. And don't you know, she did come home! Well, she's married now and Shon is alive; so I can now have my own life with Thomas. Oh, we'll not be leaving here; Sharon and Michael wish us to stay and I'm glad of that. I know it's funny for an old lady to be in the window talking to herself, but I really need to say one thing to you. Thank you both for giving me a family. Your family is the only one I have here in

America, don't you know. I'm truly grateful to you for being able to take care of Sharon and Shon. They are my own. Well, that's all I have to say. It's time for me to get married now."

I stepped back as she came out and went downstairs. I didn't want her to know I had been listening. I had no idea she gave up everything for me. I've been so selfish.

As I headed down the stairs I heard Michael saying to Maggie, "now, young lady, just where do you think you're going?"

She looked at him and the other guys with him, who were wearing their best sheepish grins and said, "I'm going to do what I do every morning. I'm going to make your breakfast and see that you are taken good care of." She proceeded toward the kitchen.

By this time I had made my way past the guys and into the kitchen and we all looked at each other and smiled. Michael gently turned Maggie around and walked her back up the stairway. "Maggie," he said, "we won't hear any of that talk from you today. This is your day and you are to go back to your room and get dressed because Sharon and I are taking you out for breakfast at the Black Dog. A couple of Thomas' friends are taking care of him on the other side of the island, so there will be no bad luck seeing the bride before the wedding. The rest of these guys will take care of things here. So, if we are going to beat the crowds we had better hurry."

Maggie didn't take orders well, but she was outnumbered. "Well, I don't know what I did to deserve such a nice treat, but I'll not argue with you. I'll be ready in a jiff! Now, don't go leaving without me. You wait right there; it'll jest take a moment to get ready. Oh my, the Black Dog, what a treat!" Then she walked into her bedroom muttering to herself under her breath, "What a day! What a blessed and special day. I feel like a queen, I do. An absolute queen."

We drove along the ocean road and as we began approaching downtown Vineyard Haven a ferry was just leaving port to go back to Woods Hole to pick up another load of eager tourists.

When we arrived at the Black Dog there was a line outside, but it wasn't as bad as it would be in another hour. It was a beautiful September day with just a little chill in the air; but even though the summer was ending, the tourists still came in droves. The shops would be having their annual "end-of-summer" sales and everyone wanted to get in on it.

It only took us ten minutes to get seated. I couldn't believe it. The waiter came over to the table and asked for our orders. I was thankful that they were serving breakfast all day because I really wanted the home fries. We all got orange juice, coffee and waffles with strawberries and whipped cream. We also got a huge order of bacon, sausages and the home fries covered in broccoli and cheese. It would be awhile until we got to eat again, besides the restaurant smelled of all the wonderful foods being cooked. How could we choose?

Maggie looked around the room and said, "You know, we used to have a time on the island when the tourists only came in the summer, now they're here all the time, don't you know. We never get the peaceful winters anymore. I miss that."

I took a sip of my coffee and said, "Yeah, I remember those times, too. Mom and Dad used to love that time of year. We could get from one point to the other without waiting in crazy traffic, there weren't long lines everywhere we went and there was a quietness that fell on the island that seemed to make the Islanders much more happy and easy going."

Michael looked towards the entrance and said, "I know, I can't believe the line out there. It isn't quite as bad as summer, but it's still pretty crowded. You know, most people don't leave the island without getting a 'Black Dog' tee shirt for everyone back home. I'd like to have a piece of those profits."

The waiter brought the food, then refilled our coffee mugs. "No more coffee for me, but I'd love a bottle of water when you get a chance."

"No problem. Be right back."

Maggie took a bite of her massive waffle smothered in cream and berries. "Oh, my, this is so delicious! Mmm, Mmm, Mmm, this is amazing. Somehow food always tastes better when someone else is doing the work for you."

It was so good to see Maggie enjoying herself and being waited on for a change. She was so involved in her feast that we didn't even bother telling her that her face was covered in whipped cream.

Afterwards we drove downtown to a gift shop. I said, "Maggie, we didn't know which piece you would select and we wanted you to have a gift that you really wanted, so Michael and I would like you to pick out your favorite piece of Belleek."

Maggie's eyes began to water, "Oh, Sharon, Michael, I just don't know what to say! I can't accept such a trophy. It's too much. You are my gift and Shon is my gift, that's enough for me."

Michael smiled at Maggie and said, "Now we'll not hear any more of that. You're worth every penny of it. You've been taking care of my Sharon her whole life. It's the very least we can do for you. A piece of pottery to remind you of Ireland."

It didn't take her long to select the piece. She had been window shopping at this place for years. She knew exactly what she wanted. "Could I have the biscuit jar? It reminds me of my mothers. Would that be too much?"

It was a beautiful piece of white Belleek, dressed in green clovers. Michael looked at the clerk and said, "The lady would like the biscuit jar. Could you wrap it for her?"

Driving home, Maggie held the box with the satin ribbon on it like it was a precious child. She looked like a little girl that just got her first doll. So happy and yet a little dreamy, she mumbled, "A queen."

"I've never had anything so pretty in my life," Maggie said. "Thank you. I can't wait to bake cookies and fill it up for you."

That was Maggie, always thinking of others. I looked at her and said, "It's about time you did have nice things, Maggie. After all, you're family." Maggie was quiet.

Back at the house Maggie went inside and Michael and I checked on the preparations in the garden. I suddenly felt nauseated. I thought I must've eaten too much. Shon and Kathie brought lots of flowers and Alcott and his daughter, Ellie were already there too. Everything looked so beautiful.

I went to see if Maggie needed help getting ready and she was in her room. She had put her gift down on the bureau next to another box, flowers and a card. I was nosily curious as she opened the card. She has a habit of reading out loud and so she read,

'A bouquet of flowers for a beautiful lady. My dear, these flowers can't touch the beauty of my Maggie. I love you my darling and can't wait to make you my bride. See you soon. Love, Thomas.'

She paused as she clutched the card to her chest and soaked it all in. Then, opening the box, Maggie discovered a treasure. "Oh my good Lord in Heaven!"

She yelled it out and it made me jump. She didn't hear me though, so I lingered to see what it was. She held up a magnificent string of pears and a pair of pearl drop earrings to match. Beautiful. There was another note with them.

'All the pearls in the sea couldn't contain the beauty of thee.'

Who knew Thomas was a poet. I almost laughed at the thought of that dear, crusty old fisherman writing poetry.

Maggie and I headed downtown to the salon to get our hair and nails done. It wasn't something Maggie really ever did, but this was her one and only wedding and it had to be very special. Her usual long braid down the back was not going to do today.

Gwen is a very well known stylist on the island and we were very lucky to have booked her at such short notice. Her salon, Gwen's Gateway, is known for amazing transformations; she calls it her gateway to beauty.

Gwen used to be my mom's hairstylist and squeezed us in as a favor to her memory.

From the time we entered the salon until the time we left, we were completely spoiled. As was the tradition, they offered tea, coffee, and croissants with raspberry jelly and butter. As we were transformed for the wedding, we listened to the upbeat gospel music she loved to play.

"Voila," Gwen said as she turned Maggie to face the mirror!

"Oh, it's beautiful. Is that me?" Maggie was very pleased with the magic the team had created with hair and makeup and she loved the nail designs they did on her fingernails and toenails. She was sparkling from head to toe with glitter, or as they called it, fairy dust.

"Next victim!" That was Gwen's usual saying whenever she finished one client and was ready for the next. It was funny.

Maggie's hairstyle gave an appearance of netting going from the top of her head to the bottom of her back. The creation was an intricate design that donned a pearl at each stopping point. My hair was simply pulled back in a ponytail, where the remainder of the tail was turned into a bow; simple, yet elegant. I got fairy dusted as well.

"Thank you so much, Gwen for taking us today, we truly appreciate it and thank you to your amazing team of technicians as well."

Maggie thanked her in turn, "You did a marvelous job with an old lady."

"Not so old, Maggie," said Gwen with a smile. "Thanks for the invite by the way, I'll be over as soon as I can get there."

Back home Maggie and I went upstairs to get dressed. I was to be her Maid-of-Honor. I picked up my shoe and handed Maggie one of hers and said, "A toast. To Mags on her wedding day. May all of your dreams come true and all of your days with Thomas be filled with happiness." We clinked shoes and had a good hug. It was nice to have this moment with her before she got lost in the crowd later.

"We better get going Mags; here, let me help you with your pearls." I clasped her necklace, threw on my shoes and headed downstairs. Maggie's getting married!

She wore a pastel blue lace dress with three quarter length sleeves. She got this at the antique store down the street and it came with a matching hat. She had had it in her closet for many years she told me, 'just in case'. She decided not to wear the hat after all because it would cover up her beautiful hairstyle.

The closer we got to the garden, the louder the music seemed. At the foot of the staircase, Michael gave Maggie one arm and me the other as he led us outside. "You two ladies look stunning. Shall we?"

I went ahead slowly and took my place next to Alcott on the gazebo. I felt so many eyes on me as I walked and I was feeling sick again, but managed a smile anyway. Then came Maggie and Michael. Thomas actually had water building behind his eyes as he held back his joy. This was the happiest day of his long life. Finally, she would be his. In his mind she always was, it was just going to be official now.

Michael led Maggie to the stairs and put her hand in Thomas' as he stepped aside to stand near me as the best man. Maggie had the look of a shy schoolgirl with a crush as she looked at her groom to be.

Alcott began, "She's a handful, Thomas, you sure you want to do this? Now's your chance." At first Maggie seemed indignant, but then she giggled, knowing he had her personality down. The crowd also found that to be very funny and the mood was instantly lifted.

Alcott continued, "Margaret and Thomas, you are about to become married in the sight of God and the close friends you have chosen as your witnesses today. The vows that you are about to say to one another are meant to seal your commitment as you hold true to each other in the sacrament of holy matrimony. Please face each other and hold hands as we proceed.

They hadn't even held hands in years and the feeling was thrilling; I could see the electricity it produced on their faces. They just lit up.

"Do you, Margaret Rose Mulcahey, take Thomas Robert Mahoney to be your husband? To be happy in the good times together and to be by his side, holding him up in the hard times throughout your marriage? Do you promise to stay by Thomas, to work together no matter how difficult things may be, never giving up on each other? Do you promise to love him even when you are temporarily parted by death and then into eternity?"

Maggie answered, "Yes, I do; for all eternity."

"Thomas, do you take Margaret to be your wife? Do you promise to watch over her and protect her from all harm? Do you promise to be the spiritual leader of your household, always being kind to your wife? Do you promise to make her happy and to always try to be understanding and compassionate in good times and in bad? And, Thomas, do you promise to love her even when you are temporarily parted by death and then into eternity?"

"Of course I do; I always have; nothing has changed that in all these years and nothing ever will."

Alcott took a step back and raised his arms towards heaven. "Thomas and Margaret, I now pronounce that you are husband and wife as God has witnessed your promises to each other. What He has put together this day, let no one dare try to take away." Then lowering his arms and looking at Maggie and

Thomas, Alcott finished with, "You may now kiss."

You can imagine what this must've felt like to Maggie since just holding hands was new to her and she was about to do this in front of everyone. Thomas grabbed her and laid one on her good. She did not seem to mind. Everyone clapped and cheered for them as they walked down into the garden. There were hugs all around.

We all really enjoyed all the food Kathie and Shon brought, then danced the night away. There was a jazz band, courtesy of Thomas' friends who played all over the island, in clubs and at outside events.

When everyone finally went home, we had some time alone with the bridge and groom. We had waited all day to give them a special gift. I handed the envelope to Maggie.

"What's this dear," asked Maggie?

"It's a gift for you and Thomas," said Michael. "Open it up."

"Oh, no, you've already given us so much," said Thomas, "we really have no need for anything else. Thank you anyway." Thomas tried to hand the envelope back to Michael.

"This is one battle you are going to lose," I said. "Open it please. It's very important to us."

"Alright, dear, thank you," Maggie said as she took the envelope. When she opened it, she gasped. Showing the contents to Thomas she said, "Oh, Sharon darling, Michael, this is too much. This is really too much." It was two round trip tickets to Ireland. "You and Michael should be taking this trip for your honeymoon; you have family there too, don't you know."

"Maggie," I broke in, "You haven't seen your sister Sheelah in nearly twenty years. I really want you to go celebrate your wedding with your family. You deserve this; you both do. You've both taken care of me and my family for so many years. Please don't ruin the moment by trying to refuse."

"You better do as she says Maggie and Thomas," began Michael. "You know how stubborn my wife can be. Besides," Michael said as he pulled out another envelope, "We're going with you!"

Maggie's eyes lit up. "Oh, I'm so excited! We're going to have so much fun! I can't wait for you to meet your aunts. Well, you know what I mean. I'm so excited I don't know what I'm saying."

Sharon chimed in, "Well, we haven't had our honeymoon yet either, remember? And it wouldn't be the same going all the way to Ireland without my family. Shon and Kathie are going too! They said they were due for a vacation. We'll have a lot of time to catch up."

"Shon and Kathie too," asked Maggie and Thomas almost simultaneously?

"How perfect," said Maggie. "I need to pack. What will I bring?"

"The trip is scheduled for September 28th, so you only have a couple of weeks to figure that out," Michael said in his teasing manner.

Maggie was so excited she couldn't wait to call her sister and tell her. She hugged everyone then grabbed Thomas. "Well, come on, husband, I have to call my sister and tell her we're coming for a visit! What a grand day we've had." She just about pulled Thomas' arm out of its socket, dragging him into the house. Let the honeymoon begin!

CHAPTER 29

Ireland or Bust

The day came when we would all leave for Ireland. Everything was all set. Alcott and Ellie would be staying at the cottage while we were gone so he could take care of Brandy and the gardens. It would be like a vacation for them since they lived in a very small apartment up island.

"Don't worry about anything, folks," said Alcott. "We'll take care of everything; you just enjoy your trip. We'll miss you."

"Miss you," called out Ellie.

"Mommy will be back soon Brandy," promised Maggie through tears. She absolutely hated leaving him. They hadn't been separated since he was a pup. "I need to be going now, but I'll be back boy." Maggie was a mess by the time she got in the car from all the sobbing.

Everyone else was already loaded into the limo that would take us to the airport.

We headed to the Island airport where we would take the first leg of our trip. There would be several changeovers along the way and this would be only the beginning. We were all very excited and talked up a storm all the way to Logan Airport, where we would board another plane.

There were movies shown on the larger airlines and Maggie and Thomas amused themselves with a card game for awhile. It was a very long flight indeed, but with the meals and movies it went by a little faster than I had anticipated. Soon we dropped off one at a time and napped for awhile. When I woke up we were landing on the beautiful

Emerald Isle. The view as we land is spectacular.

It was quite a site from the air. Everyone was leaning in to look out the windows. The lush, green grass seemed endless. As the plane drew closer to the ground I could see cottages covered in ivy and flowers, and farmland for miles on the outskirts of the airport. This was promising to be a great vacation.

Maggie was so excited to see her sister that she almost didn't wait for the plane to land as she grabbed for her carry-on. She was ready to bolt for the door.

When we entered the airport, Maggie dropped her bags and ran into the middle of a crowd. I lost sight of her. Then I heard her calling out, "Sheelah!"

When we caught up to her she was embracing a woman I could only guess must be her sister. "Maggie," said Michael, "we thought we lost you there for a minute, you took off so fast."

"I'm sorry Michael dear, I couldn't wait to get to Sheelah. This is my baby sister. Sheelah, this is my Sharon and her dear husband, Michael."

"I'm so pleased to meet you both. I hear you're a Doctor, Michael. That's fine, it is. And, Sharon, my dear, sweet, Sharon." I didn't even know this woman and she was crying as she met me, like we were long, lost family or something. What a sweet welcome. I guess that's how the Irish are.

Maggie chimed in, "Sharon is carrying a wee one, don't you know. It's very exciting!"

"What," I exclaimed in shock?! "What are you talking about Maggie?! I'm not pregnant!"

"Sure you are darling," said Maggie as Michael looked confused. "Why do you think you've been so sick lately? Mostly in the morning, right? And I've never seen you eat as much as you have lately sweetie. Not to mention the fact that you had red peppers on your salad the other night. You hate red peppers!"

"Oh my goodness," I began, "you're right! I hate red peppers. I didn't even realize I was eating any different. But I've been eating them with practically every meal lately and I thought I was just hungry because of the excitement and nerves of getting married. Do you really think....?" I looked down and gently stroked my belly.

Michael wrapped his arms around me instantly and kissed me on the cheek. "Oh, my darling, it's a dream come true. I love you." Then he leaned over and kissed my belly. "I love you," he said to our baby.

"I love you too, Michael," I said with melancholy in my voice. "But we don't know anything for sure yet." My life, which was on hold for so many years was suddenly catapulted into high gear. First my marriage, then Shon coming home, then Maggie getting married, and now this. I took a deep breath.

Everyone started celebrating. "Congratulations Sharon and Michael," said Sheelah. "I can't wait to be getting to know you better. Maggie talks of nothing else but her family on 'the other island'."

"This is my Shon and his dear wife, Kathie and this is my Thomas," Maggie said, continuing the introductions.

"Well, Thomas, you'll have to be telling me how you finally got my stubborn sister to say yes to marriage. She shoulda done it long ago, don't you know. And Shon,"

Sheelah said as she hugged him tight, "I'm so happy to be hearing you're ok and that you've found your family again. What a hard time that was for you all. Welcome to the family, Kathie. Now, let's get out of this stuffy airport and off to my home. There's a whole houseful of folks waiting for us. Sharon, some of your relatives are here also don't you know. They can't wait to be seeing you."

And with that, we all got into Sheelah's truck with all the luggage. There almost wasn't enough room for all of us. Sheelah, Maggie and I crowded into the cab, while the rest of them got in the back of the pickup with the mound of luggage. It wasn't far, so no one seemed to mind. As we drove away from the airport and headed into the country we saw many beautiful sights. The river seemed to follow us all the way and the hillsides were magical as the dew shone from the sunlight.

We arrived with a jerk as Sheelah slammed on the brakes. The chickens were loose and running across the road. A group of seven ladies, dressed in housedresses and aprons came out the door raising their hands in joyful anticipation of the many hugs they were about to give us. Some had wooden spoons in their hands, showing that they were cooking when we arrived and didn't bother putting them down before running out of the house. Others were waiving loaves of bread. One woman even had a chicken in mid-pluck dangling by its legs in her capable hands. It was quite a sight.

There were four men in tow, dressed in woolen trousers, boots, suspenders and shirts with rolled up sleeves. Two of the men were smoking pipes and one, what appeared to be a home-rolled cigarette. The men were following as ordered by the women calling back to them. One man was rolling a barrel out and set it up in the middle of the yard, pouring beer into mugs and offering them to us. These were extremely friendly people! Now I know where Maggie gets her energy.

Sheelah hopped right out of the truck and we all followed. She began shooing the chickens and grabbed a pint for herself, downing it like a man and slamming the mug down on the barrel. It was utter chaos and it was great. The men got all the luggage and brought it inside after awhile. Michael and Shon tried to help Sheelah's husband, John with the bags, but were quickly told otherwise. "Don't you go taking my job away from me lad. My lovely wife will have my head if I let a guest do any work, don't you know. You can escort your pretty wives insides and warm them by the fire."

It was pretty funny watching the men throw around all that testosterone. As long as I didn't have to carry it all, they could do anything they wanted.

Thomas said to Sheelah, "Thank you for letting us all invade your home."

Sheelah put her hands on her hips and said, "You're not invading anything. You're family. Now, that will be enough of that."

I looked all around, taking in the beauty of this lush land. Their beautiful stone house sat on the lake and it was massive. Most of the homes in this area are small, but I could tell this one had been added on to over the years. There was an amazing vegetable garden around the back that could feed a small army and besides the chickens, there were goats and cows. A true working farm. I was in heaven.

Sheelah noticed me looking dreamily at the layout and came over. "'Tis a beautiful thing isn't it? God has blessed this place. We have a saying in these parts. *God created the heavens and the earth and then turned his head in this direction, let out a breath of life on this land and smiled upon it.*"

"Beautiful," I said.

Inside the cabin the festivities had begun. The man who wanted me to call him Uncle Jim was playing his guitar and singing, 'Wild Rover' and everyone joined in. I truly love all the old Irish songs. I used to play my guitar and sing them with my mother. She would love this.

Dinner was ready and I was hungry, as usual. The aromas coming from the kitchen were pure torture. The chickens being plucked earlier, it turns out, would be for tomorrow's lunch. Tonight we would feast on lamb, colcannon and fresh corn from their own garden. Colcannon was familiar to me since Maggie made it for special occasions.

Although there are many alternatives to this dish, Maggie made hers with mashed potatoes, shredded cabbage, leeks, butter, salt and pepper.

There was a lot of Irish soda bread, which I dearly love and gobs of what could only be freshly churned butter, courtesy of the cows in the yard. Irish butter that I get at home is wonderful, but I've never had it fresh from the source. I'm actually quite excited for this meal.

Around the tables sat Thomas, Maggie, Sheelah and John; Shon, Kathie, Michael and myself. Also joining the feast were a handful of my cousins whom I didn't even know existed; Maureen and Matthew along with their ten year old son, Jack to name a few. Mary Lou and Stephen were Maggie's niece and nephew; Irene and Donald, who were my aunt and Scottish uncle, whom I also knew nothing of; Mary Kate and Paul, and finally Kathleen and Frank; all Maggie's cousins. If there's a test at the end of the night I will surely fail. I'm terrible at remembering names.

There were pints of guiness at each table, courtesy of Frank who had a small brewery in town, but the smell of it was nauseating me. Everyone was enjoying themselves so much that after dinner they wanted to go to the pub.

There were so many people running to us as they saw Sheelah come in. She was obviously a regular. Some of Maggie's old friends had been told she was heading that way and met her there as well. She was thrilled to see them after all these years.

Michael and I danced on the small wooden floor and as we held each other close Michael whispered in my ear. "I'm so happy about the baby, Sharon. We haven't had any time to talk about that alone. But I just wanted you to know that I'm truly happy. Truly."

He continued, "Do you remember the Irish Village? Who would have guessed, looking back on that night, that we would end up here? Married, having a baby and in Ireland."

I kissed him straight on the mouth. I kissed him hard and I kissed him long. "Mr. Brennan, thank you for loving me enough for both of us, until I came to my senses. Isn't this place great? I know we're just visiting and all, but I feel so close to these people; as if I've known them my whole life. I know it's silly, but I can't shake the feeling."

"I know, everyone has been so warm and kind to us." Michael looked over at Sheelah and her husband, dancing. "Look at them. They've been together since they were kids and they act like newlyweds. That's going to be us. We're always going to love each other like that."

Kathie and Shon were sitting at the table just taking everything in and relaxing after the long trip while Thomas and Maggie stood by the doorway talking to someone I hadn't met. They came over towards us on the dance floor.

"Looks like you two are having a grand time together," said Maggie, "but we've got to interrupt you for a minute. Michael, you will never guess who this man is." Michael looked at the man and saw that he looked familiar; strangely familiar.

"Michael dear, you'll never believe this, but this is your daddy's cousin, Kevin from Galway. His name is Kevin Brennan."

Kevin shook Michael's hand and said, "'Tis a pure pleasure to be meetin' one o' me own from the states, it is. I was jest standin' over there taking pictures for a mag and I happened on this pub for a wee pint. These lovely people started talking to me about your visit here for your honeymoon and I asked your name. When I heard Brennan my ears perked. After awhile we figured the truth of our connection to each other. Welcome to Ireland, Cousin Michael."

Stories were passed around all night, connecting Michael with his family and me with mine, while I learned more of Maggie's. It was fascinating.

It got to be quite late and I was overtired by this point. I was ready for bed long ago but didn't want to be rude to our hosts. Michael and Kevin exchanged information and he promised to visit us in the states next year. Our group was a never ending bundle of energy, even at this hour, but Michael and I dragged ourselves out the door, down the hill and after being shown to our room, fell into our beds, exhausted.

This is a magical place filled with joy.

CHAPTER 30

Prince August's Soldier Factory

Michael and I slept in, only to rise at around noon. We went downstairs and found the family cleaning up from lunch. "Good morning everyone," I said happily.

"Morning," said Sheelah? "You've slept half the day away, you did. 'Tis 12:30 in the afternoon. I slept a little late myself this morning. I didn't rise until 7:00. Come. Sit down and have some food now."

"We had such a wonderful time yesterday with all of you," I said. "I can hardly wait to see what today brings. Are there any plans?"

"Well Sharon darling," began Maggie, "we thought we'd be taking you to see some of the sights."

"That sounds wonderful. What will we see," I asked?

"Well," added John, "we thought you might like to head to Garnish Island or St. Ann's Shandon to ring the famous bells or maybe even to the Skellig Rocks off o' the Kerry coast to see the seabirds and lighthouse, or..."

Sheelah broke in, "Sharon dear, don't feel overwhelmed with the likes o' that man's talk. You'll be here for three weeks and we don't want to be wearing you out like a pair of old shoes. John over there kissed the Blarney Stone some thirty years ago and he's been talking the hind leg off of a donkey ever since."

"I think Sharon and Shon would love to go to Prince August's Toy Soldier Factory," said Maggie. "It's right here in Cork."

"Maggie," said Shon teasingly, "we're all grown up now, I don't play with toy soldiers anymore."

"Don't you think I'd be knowing that smarty pants," asked Maggie? "But 'tis not just toy soldiers they'll be making there. These figures cover from the Nativity scene to Chess pieces and Christmas ornaments. Sharon, you'd be liking the kits they sell."

"Kits," I asked with excitement? "Like the kind I can take home and paint my own?"

"It's not just painting, darlin'," said John. "Do you see that chess set over there? I made every piece on that board from scrap metal. I melted it all myself and filed and painted to perfection. I got the molds and everything I needed at Prince August. I'm on to making a Nativity set next. I need to pick up some things while we're there. You in?"

Shon and I answered in unison, "Let's go!"

And with that, we all headed out. I was so excited. I was hoping we could see a demonstration. I knew I'd have to buy a kit and try it out for myself.

When we got there the building was magnificent. There was a painting on the whole front of it which depicted a battle between man and dragon around a castle. Inside was indescribable. There were toy soldiers and other casts set up in battle scenes, country outings, chess sets and more. I could've spent an entire day in there and still never seen everything there was to see.

They were having a demonstration, which I was very excited about and while a few of us watched that, others shopped. Watching how the metal just melted into pure liquid in seconds, was poured into molds and within five minutes became a solid mass again, was fascinating. They then took the piece out of the mold, brushed it with a metal brush to remove the powder they had put in the mold to prevent air bubbles, filed the base then set aside. The brushing left the piece shiny. After that process is done they opt to paint the piece or leave it silver.

There was an area where they were allowing people to make a toy soldier with their supervision and take it home. I could not pass that up. John and Michael joined me in that festivity and we had so much fun. I was afraid I would pour all the hot metal all over the place, but with their instruction it seemed almost easy. I couldn't wait to get my own supplies to take home.

I bought everything I needed to make a medieval chess set and Michael got the Nativity kit as well as the Christmas tree ornament set for us to share. It would be a great memory to have and something we could hand down to our children. Our children. I couldn't help but smile at the thought that I may be carrying Michael's child.

After the toy soldier factory, we decided to stop at the English Market. Although Sheelah made the most amazing bread for us and we got to sample some cheeses from her cows and goats, I wanted to see what else Cork had to offer.

The market was great. There were cheeses from all over the county and the smell of bread wafting through the air was intoxicating. One booth sold an assortment of marmalades, some of which I had never heard of. I got the grapefruit and the lime. Then we picked up some bread with meat in it and some with fruit. Some cheese was aged, while others were fresh and soft, made that very morning. We would have a taste testing when we got back.

Our group arrived back at the house and sat in front of the fire for awhile. It was nice to rest after running around all day. We had tea and all the wonderful foods we got at the market as well as some dried meats John had made. I don't think I can take that stuff on the plane, but I've never tasted dried sausage this good before and it went so well with the fruit bread and cheese.

"I'm so glad you finally married Thomas, Maggie," said Sheelah out of the blue.

"Me too, Sheelah; me too. He's a wonderful man he is and so is your John. I really like him. I'm most thankful today for you and Sharon and Michael and for Kathie and

Shon as well. Especially my Shon baby. We missed him so," said Maggie. "I can't believe he's alive and God has give him back to us. It's a miracle it is."

"That's so true Maggie dear," said John. "And having you all here is a miracle too. We never thought we'd be seeing the likes of you again. It's been too long."

"'Tis a happy day," said Maggie. "No tears now. I won't be having it," she said as Sheelah's eyes dampened.

"You're right Maggie. I'm just so happy to see you is all."

CHAPTER 31

Cronin's Irish Pub

Everyone was on time for breakfast today because they were drawn to the aromas wafting upwards from the kitchen below. The bacon, oh the bacon! These people got their bacon from a neighboring pig farm and it was the best I've ever had. It hit my senses first then the bread and, as always, coffee. There was plenty more, but those were the first things I smelled.

Maggie was helping prepare the meal as she turned to see Shon coming in alone. "Good morning sunshine," she said to him. "Where's your lovely bride?"

Shon yawned and said, "Good morning everyone. Kathie is feeling a little under the weather so I told her I'd bring her up some tea and toast, if that's okay."

"Oh, the poor dear. You just sit yourself down now and I'll be bringing up a tray for her," Maggie said.

Shon knew better than to argue with Maggie, so he sat down and thanked her. "Did anyone ever tell you that you're wonderful, Mags?"

Maggie blushed and pushed his shoulder saying, "Ah, g'wan with ya now. Eat your breakfast." Then, as she prepared the tray for Kathie, "Always the charmer."

Michael and I were sitting together at one end of the table and got into the conversation that had already been booming through it all. "Michael and I were looking through some brochures of the area and there's a restaurant we'd like to take you and Maggie to Thomas. Would you like that?"

Maggie, now walking back into the room nodded to Thomas and said, "Well, you've spoiled us so much now, that we were just saying that we'd like to be taking you two out. So, we'll agree to the restaurant you chose only if we can treat."

Michael put his hands up in the air in mock defeat. "You win. We'll take you to dinner at Cronin's Irish Pub in Crosshaven and you can pay."

Maggie felt proud and raised her cup. "A toast. To dinner at the Pub."

Sheelah laughed at all of them. It was so much fun having the house filled with family. "Well, I'll tell you one thing, it's a good place to go on a cold, rainy day like today. It's nice and warm there and the food is the finest you'll have. Their specialty is the open brown sandwiches. You'll never have to eat again since they give you so much food. Don't forget to leave room for the desserts though. They have the most delicious bread n' butter pudding and a death by chocolate dessert. You simply must try a little of both."

Thomas said, "Well, sounds like you picked a very nice restaurant kids. I can't wait to try it. Sheelah, would you and John like to join us tonight?"

"No, thank you anyway Thomas, it's sweet of you to ask, but John and I just want to stay in and rest a bit. We have plenty of time to go out while you're here. Take our car to the restaurant and any time you'd like while you're here."

"Thank you, Sheelah. You've all made us feel so at home since we arrived," said Sharon. "We're never going to want to leave."

"That's fine with us sweetie. There's always room for more family," added John.

Shon decided to stay back as well, to keep Kathie company. He didn't want to leave her alone in a strange place.

Around 6:00 that night we headed down the twelve-mile stretch to the town of Crosshaven and to Cronin's Irish Pub for supper.

It was a large brick building with pretty lights in the windows. The pub was very clean and comfortable with subdued lighting and dark wood. There are stories that the pub even has its own ghost.

We were seated and had ordered our drinks; ale for Maggie, Thomas and Michael and Water for me. After looking over the menu, I decided to start with the seafood chowder, which was laced with brandy and cream. The brandy, I was told is cooked out during the cooking process, so I was okay with that.

When the chowder arrived it was accompanied by another round of beer, which the others did not order, and a pretty pink, sugary, non-alcoholic drink for me. The waitress pointed towards the bar and said, "Ray said the drinks are on the house. John called ahead and told us to take real good care of his family." Thomas waived to Ray and asked the waitress to thank him. Ray is not only the head barman, but also great friends with John and Sheelah as they frequent Cronin's.

Maggie tasted the chowder and said, "This is so delicious." Thomas agreed as did everyone else, since they all ordered it once they saw mine.

Later the waitress came by to clear the dishes for the next course. Most of us ordered the brown sandwiches on Sheelah's recommendation. Maggie got the ham cooked in cider. Thomas' was the roast chicken and Michael and I each got the Crab Mayonnaise sandwiches; all on toasted brown bread.

Can I just tell you that brown bread in Ireland is definitely not the brown bread we get in a can here in America. Although I like brown bread in a can, with raisins, warmed, with butter, it's a whole different animal when it's fresh.

After stuffing our faces, dessert arrived. How I would fit in another bite was beyond me, but this was, after all, vacation, so what the heck. Our waitress, Bernadette, brought two bread 'n butter puddings and two death by chocolates to share. Irish coffee of course accompanied the desserts, mine was without the

Irish. We lingered awhile before waddling back to the truck.

CHAPTER 32

A Haunting

The next few days were spent seeing the local sites and eating more great food. Kathie decided her illness must be the flu and spent her time in bed. Maggie and Sheelah took turns taking care of her, insisting that Shon get out of the house for awhile.

It was 3:00 in the morning when all were woken suddenly by a blood curdling scream. It was coming from inside me! Maggie and Thomas were staying in the next room and were the first to get to me. I was sitting up in bed and Michael was trying to comfort me by putting his arms around me.

"Heavens, child," started Maggie. "Whatever is it?!"

That's what I'm trying to find out now Maggie," said Michael. "What is it, Sharon? Were you having a nightmare? Are you okay, sweetie?"

Through broken breaths, I managed to say, "ghost, I saw a ghost!"

"Oh," began Sheelah who had just overheard what was said, "You're probably having a bad dream, darling, that's all. There's never been a ghost in this house in all the years I have lived here, and that's a considerable amount of time, don't you know. Why don't you come downstairs and we'll talk about it."

Before going downstairs, Michael wrapped the blanket around me since I was shivering uncontrollably and said, "Tell us about your dream honey."

"It wasn't a dream I tell you. I saw a ghost! It was standing right in front of me. A woman wearing a plain white dress with an old gray cape, tied at the neck. She was standing right where you are now!" I pointed towards Kathie, who just arrived and she drew back in fear.

Then, as we headed downstairs, I continued, "She had the hood of the cape up, covering her head and I could just make out her face. She was lovely. Her long black hair was styled in ringlets, which fell from inside the hood, and her skin was in direct contrast, appearing porcelain-like. The thing that scared me the most, though, was when I noticed that she had one blue eye and one green. It was frightening, yet familiar somehow."

Just then Sheelah fainted. "Good Lord," stated John, "now what's wrong with Sheelah? Has this whole house gone crazy tonight? Sheelah," began John while gently tapping her cheek, "wake up, darling."

Hearing John's voice, Sheelah came to and was as white as the ghost I had just described. "What is it," I asked? "I hope I didn't frighten you."

Then Sheelah looked around the room at her family and got the courage to utter one word, "Mum!"

"No, Sheelah," demanded Maggie. "That can't be who she saw. I know it sounds like her, and I don't know too many people who have two different colored eyes, but I'll not be believing in spooks. Besides, Mom has been dead for twenty-five years now. If she was going to come back, why not years ago and why would she show herself to Sharon? What makes you think it's Mum?"

"Maggie," began Sheelah, once she caught her breath. "I've been seeing things around the house; strange things, indeed. Mom's picture over the mantle, just the other day, before you all came here, 'twas watching me, I tell you. Then I heard Mum's voice in the kitchen and saw one of her old dresses lying on the couch. I thought I was going crazy, I did!"

"Wait a minute," I interrupted. "You mean, the woman I saw, matches the description of your mother?"

"Yes, it does," said Sheelah. "Haven't you seen her picture over the hearth in there?" Sheelah indicated the living room direction.

"Well, I saw a picture, but I didn't really look closely at it," I said as I got up to go into the living room. I looked up at the picture and someone switched on the light, which shone directly on the woman's face. I jumped a mile. "It's her," I cried! "It's the woman in the bedroom! I'm so not sleeping in there tonight."

"But why," asked John, "would she be haunting this house? And why now, after all these years?" That seemed to be the question on everyone's mind.

"Yes," I added, "and I agree with Maggie's question about why she would reveal her presence to me, a stranger. I never met her in all my life."

"I wish I knew the answers to all of those questions, but alas I don't," said John. "All I know is that the room you're staying in was hers. The very room she laid to rest for the last time. She died in her sleep, peacefully."

Well, no one could sleep now, since we were all spooked and decided to stay up and have a very early breakfast. I was famished, as usual. We all had our fill as the sun came up over the hills. It was a beautiful view through the window that morning and we decided on a walk around the lake to calm ourselves and work off all the food we had been eating.

By the time we returned from our walk I was feeling a bit weak, which was so unlike me, so I decided to go lay down. It was still daytime, so I wasn't afraid to go upstairs alone, nevertheless, Michael insisted on sitting in the room until I fell asleep, which didn't take very long, since we had gotten up so early. In fact, Michael, exhausted as he was, fell asleep in the chair beside the bed just seconds before I closed my eyes and fell into a deep sleep.

I dreamt of a woman. The woman in the picture. Her name, revealed to me in the dream, was Teresa and she was trying to show me something. There was something hidden in the house that Teresa wanted found. So, in the dream I followed her. I was guided out of the bedroom, down the stairs, out the back door and through the gardens. There was a bench there that was overgrown with ivy and hadn't been occupied in years. Teresa stood there and pointed towards the bench, insistently. Then, as I turned to ask her what she wanted me to do, she vanished.

I awoke suddenly from my dream and went over to Michael to wake him up as well.

"Michael, I need to go outside. Will you come with me?"

"Of course, but why?"

"I had a dream about the woman, her name is Teresa, and she was trying to show me something in the garden."

"It was just a dream, Sharon; don't worry about it."

I became agitated as I blurted out, "Oh, never mind, Michael! I'll go myself!"

"No, I'll go with you." Michael seemed confused and worried. "Just let me put on some shoes first."

Heading outside I lead the way to where the lady had brought me in my dream; out the back door, through the kitchen, around the bend and into the overgrown garden. "There it is! I knew it!" We had found the bench I saw in my dream. It did exist. The one the lady was so insistent on showing me. "See, I told you. Now how else would I have known this bench was out here? It's covered in vines. The bench is exactly where I knew it would be."

"Ok, so now what," asked Michael, curiously?

"Something about the bench," I told him, remembering the dream as I spoke, in order to do exactly what the lady wanted me to do. "In the dream, Teresa was pointing at the bench. She wanted me to find something there. She seemed to be pointing under the bench, but I'm not really sure."

"What do you mean, under the bench? The only things under there are more weeds, Sharon. Maybe she was pointing to the bench. But why?"

"I don't know, Michael. I just know that there's something so important out here that Teresa came back from the dead to tell us about it and then crept into my dreams to make sure I would find it."

I moved some of the vines away from the bench and felt my way around the top and back of the seat. There was nothing that Michael or I could see on the surface, so we moved more of the vines and weeds away, in order to look further.

"Ok, maybe there's something under the bench. I'll look," said Michael as he knelt down and actually crawled in the mud, to get a better look underneath the rotting love seat. "There's nothing here," he called out from among the weeds and mud. He came back up too fast and bumped his head on the underside of the seat. He didn't think he hit that hard, but it really hurt as if it was a rock he slammed into, he told me.

Just then a hidden trap door fell open, revealing a tin box, which dropped to the ground with a splat into the muck. Michael looked up at me and I back at him. The world seemed to stop in that moment.

We couldn't believe our eyes. This couldn't be real. It was all way too strange. Teresa, a woman who had been dead these past twenty years, decides to come back from the dead while we're visiting and spring some kind of surprise on us. We were almost afraid to pick up the box. It laid there in the mud for what seemed an eternity before I finally reached down and picked it up.

I held it away from my body as if it was a bomb because it was dripping in muck and it was sent to us by a dead woman! Michael was entranced with the sight of the object as well. Maybe shocked is more like it, which ever, neither one of us could even conceive what was happening.

"Let's clean it off under the hose over here, Michael; then we can bring it inside. We need to open it with the family. After all, we're just guests here and this doesn't belong to us. No one's going to believe that Teresa told me about this in a dream, though. And I wouldn't blame them if they thought I was nuts. I know I would, if the tables were turned." I was nervous about approaching the others about this.

Nonetheless, we cleaned off the box and went inside to tell our story to the others. Everyone was home now and sitting at the kitchen table, having tea and homemade cookies. After explaining what had happened, and while the box lay dormant on the table before us, John got an ice pick to pry it open.

The box was made of hand hammered tin, with the Celtic cross design chiseled around the edges. Sheelah recognized the box as her mother's sewing box, which her dad had made for her as a wedding gift. It was meant for jewelry, but, as Sheelah explained, her mother was much too practical for such extravagances. It was decades old, according to Maggie and had survived at least the twenty-five years since their mother had passed, in Ireland's inclement weather.

John put the ice pick between the lock and the box and pried it open with one quick movement. It wasn't difficult, giving the rust that had accumulated on the lock itself. For some strange reason though, the box was in great condition. John removed the lock and stepped back. We all just stared at it.

"Good Lord," said Maggie. "Go on and open it, Sheelah. What's the sense in prolonging the suspense."

Sheelah looked at Maggie and asked, "Are you sure? We don't have to look inside, Mag's. It's up to you."

There were a lot of confused looks going around the table. No one knew what to make of that conversation. Why wouldn't Maggie want the box opened? It was probably just a treasured trinket or love letters. What was the big deal?

"Open it," was all Maggie said as she looked at Sheelah. Then, anticipating her next question added, "I'm sure."

A shiver seemed to go through the room as Sheelah opened the box. No one breathed. No one spoke. And unbeknownst to the family, Teresa stood among us. There were papers in the box, yellowed with age, but otherwise untouched. Sheelah unrolled the papers as they were in a scroll and tied with a red ribbon. A few pieces broke off of the edges as she carefully opened the delicate treasure. In this moment I realized that the box must've had an incredible seal to keep the papers from being wet. Sheelah read the note, at first to herself, looking quite troubled as she read.

"What is it, Sheelah, darling," Maggie asked?

"Well, they're legal documents and it says here that... well, Mag's it says here that..."

"Well, what does it say there," asked John quickly?!

Maggie looked on in horror as the truth was revealed. Sheelah began.

To whomever shall read these words, know that they are true and honest. In the presence of my lawyer I write that I have two beautiful daughters by the names of Sheelah and Margaret.

I also write that my dearest Margaret...

Maggie suddenly looked frightened and defeated as she looked at Sheelah and nodded her head for her to continue.

Sheelah continued where she left off.

I also write that my dearest Margaret also has a daughter by the give name, Anna Ciera.

All eyes shifted towards Maggie at once only to find her looking down, seemingly ashamed and relieved at the same time. You see, Anna Ciera was my mother's name.

That wasn't to be the whole letter, though, we realized as Sheelah continued.

Whosoever finds this I pray you do not use it to harm my daughter or her family in any way, but rather to help them to know the truth and embrace it.

Lovingly signed,

Teresa Rose Mulcahey

All eyes were now glued on Maggie. Especially mine and Shon's. "Is it true, Maggie," I asked? "What does this mean? That you are our... grandmother? How can that be after all these years? You're our housekeeper!"

"Sharon," yelled Shon, shocked at my indifference to Maggie's feelings at this very tender moment. "Maggie is far more than a housekeeper. You and I both know that!"

"I'm sorry, Shon. I'm so sorry, Maggie," I said, coming to my senses. I felt ripped off at that moment. I had a grandmother all these years and didn't know it. I wondered what it would've been like had I known. "You know I didn't mean it that way; at least I hope you know how much you mean to me, to us. I just don't know what to say right now."

"It's alright dear," explained Maggie. "I understand. This is going to take some time to sink in." Maggie sat down not knowing what else to say. Thomas came over and put his hand on her shoulder and spoke for her.

"Sharon, Shon, it's true, my doves. Maggie is your grandmother. She had relations when she was not married and it was not heard of back then, a woman with no husband. There would be great shame on her and her family, so her mother decided to protect her. She was sent away to a convent to have her child, your Mum, in secret.

Teresa was a very good woman and she asked a family called O'Callahan to raise her granddaughter, Anna. Maggie agreed to this if she was allowed to remain on with the O'Callahan family as their housekeeper, so she could help to raise the wee one. And I," said Thomas with his head bowed, "agreed to the arrangement as long as I could be the gardener in my daughter's new home."

There was a gasp from Sheelah, for up until this very moment she had not known who the father was. Maggie had always protected his name. I was feeling dizzy with all this information coming so quickly and unexpectedly. I took a seat and started to calm myself.

"You're telling me... that you..." stuttered Shon, in spurts, "Maggie... and you.... Thomas... You're telling me that you are mine and Sharon's grandparents?!"

Shaken, Maggie replied, "Yes, that we are, darling'"

"Why," I wanted to know, "have you kept this from us? From Mom! Oh, my God in heaven, Mom! She died never knowing who her real mother was. How awful for her. Maggie, Thomas, you could've told us. Don't you know we love you like family?"

"We were ashamed of what we had done, dear," Thomas said. "Now you know why I wanted to marry Maggie so. I didn't want her feeling bad anymore of what we did. I proposed as soon as I found out, but Maggie didn't want to marry me. You see, she had already begun to show before we knew."

"There's nothing to feel bad about Maggie," I managed to say once I put my own feelings aside. I ran to her side and hugged her. "I only wish I knew all these years who you two were! I'm so sorry we had you both working for us when you should've been part of the family. Oh, I love you so much! I love you both."

Then Shon and I mischievously spoke, one finishing the other's sentence. "So, do we call you Nana and Papa now or what?"

"I wish you would darling," said Maggie, with tears streaming down her face. She didn't expect such acceptance from her grandchildren. After all, her and Thomas had robbed them of the best years of their lives with grandparents. "'Tis what I've longed to hear all my days; that and Mum! I've missed out on that, but perhaps it's not too late for us."

CHAPTER 33

Another Surprise?!

The next morning, as I stepped out onto the porch, I saw Thomas standing there, smelling the fresh morning air and admiring the beautiful view of the glens, touched by the morning dew. The sky was just beginning to clear. He seemed to have such a peace about him. I couldn't begin to imagine the pain he and Maggie had endured, keeping such a huge secret all those years. Then I thought, 'Papa', and I walked up to him and gave him a soft kiss on the cheek. "Good morning, Papa," I said with a smile on my face that I could not remove since the night before. "How would you like to take your granddaughter for a walk? It's a beautiful morning."

Thomas had little wrinkles around his eyes and when he smiled, the creases deepened and showed the kindness behind them. He took my hand in his and gave it a little pat. "'T'would be my greatest pleasure, Rosie, darling, to walk with you this fine morning. That is if you don't mind going slow for an old man."

"There's nothing old about you, Thomas...Papa."

When Thomas and I came back from our stroll along the water's edge, breakfast was ready and everyone was already at the table beginning to eat.

Kathie came down for breakfast this morning too, although she wasn't too sure just how much she could get down. She was still feeling queasy. Michael observed how frail she looked again and said, "Kathie, after breakfast, why don't you and I go upstairs and I'll give you a quick check up?"

I was sure Kathie was willing to try anything to end this nausea she had been having. She answered Michael saying, "Thanks, I'd appreciate that."

After breakfast, Michael and I went upstairs with Kathie. He examined her and asked some questions. Then he went to get Shon. Shon stopped short at the entrance to the bedroom, almost afraid to go in, when he saw Kathie sitting in a chair by the window smiling at him. Shon had been so worried about his wife's sudden illness.

He walked over to her. "What is it, Kath?" I stepped aside so he could give her a hug.

"Nothing's wrong, Shon. You and I are going to have a baby! I'm just having a really bad first trimester is all."

"Tri what? You're serious! Kathie, you're not kidding me are you?" Kathie was answering in nods and shakes of her head as Shon babbled on when suddenly he swooped her up out of her chair and swung her around in circles, almost dancing with her. He was so relieved that nothing was seriously wrong with her that he couldn't contain himself. Then, "Oh, you better sit down Hon, I'm sorry, I shouldn't be picking you up. Oh my giddy aunt! I mean, thank you, Lord! This is a great Day!" Kathie laughed at him, then ran to the bathroom to throw up.

I joined Michael who was in the kitchen, drinking some coffee. People were up in arms trying to get answers out of him. They kept asking if anything was wrong with Kathie because they were all so concerned; especially when Shon ran up to see her. Michael nonchalantly picked up a piece of cinnamon toast and took a bite with a wide grin plastered on his face. He looked around the table, noticing all the curious faces and said, "What? Hasn't anyone ever heard of Doctor-Patient confidentiality?

Shon and Kathie came in just then. Shon scanned the suddenly quieted room just to hold the suspense in the air a little bit longer before he made the announcement. "Kathie's just fine everyone. She's just a little.... well, she's a little bit..."

"Oh, good Lord," said Kathie. "I'm pregnant! There will be one more added to this fine family."

"Two," I said, holding my still quite flat belly.

There were congratulations and cheers all around. Maggie said, "Good Lord above, Thomas. We're going to have two great-grandchildren at the same time.

This is wonderful, it is. God bless and keep you, my loves." Then she went over to the happy parents and hugged the life out of us all.

Everyone else followed suit and I added, "Your news is so great. Our children will grow up together, just as Shon and I did. What a blessing. I only wish Mom and Dad could be with us. They would have been so happy to be grandparents. Now you two have to get off of Nantucket and move back home to Martha's Vineyard. I want our kids to be close. As close as we always were, Shon, and always will be."

Shon and Kathie had a lucrative business going on Nantucket, but after all, they could cook anywhere. They looked at each other, curiously as Shon said, "funny you should mention it, but we've already talked about that. The day I found out who I truly was, was the day I felt a strong draw to be with you all. We already put the house on the market."

John piped in with, "Well, there you go again, now we really have some celebrating to do. Babies, family moving near family and Thomas and Maggie being grandparents and now, great-grandparents. Aye, 't'will be a fine party, it will."

Sheelah added, "any excuse to pour a pint. I do agree however, this is indeed a time for celebrating. A wee one on the way; two wee ones on the way. I'll fix a party up for tonight and call a few more friends over. Oh, what a night we'll have. We've so much to be thankful for, we do."

While the ladies were baking and preparing for the party, John saw his chance to get away. I heard him say, "It feels like a lucky day to me men, what do you say we grab a few poles and go catch some mackerel down at the river for dinner."

They needed no coaxing to get lost while the women did all the work. So without hesitation they all went out to the shed and picked up the poles and the worm can and hightailed it out of here before the women could put them to work.

I never liked the segregation of women and men with the mentality that the women cook and clean while the men sit on the couch and watch a game, or in this case, go fishing, so I grabbed a pole and ran after them.

CHAPTER 34

Gone Fishin'

Thomas cast his rod into the water and turned to Shon. "You know Shon, things have been happening so fast with the trip and all, I haven't really had the chance to tell you how happy I am that we've found you again. Your Nana said prayers for you every night and I did my share of praying too, and here you are, standing before my very eyes and I still can't believe what I see. The good Lord answered our prayers, Shon. We love you and Sharon with all our hearts. I just wanted you to know that lad."

Shon looked out at the rushing river, the cool breeze blowing in his thick, auburn hair and began to cry. I had never seen him cry before. It was halting. I guess so much had happened to us all in such a short amount of time that he couldn't hold back his pure joy and thankfulness any longer.

He looked at Thomas, laid his arm on his shoulder and said, "Papa, I love you too. I've never been so happy in my whole life, that I can remember. Just when I think that a moment couldn't get any better than the one I'm having, something else happens that tops it. This is one of those moments for me and I'll treasure this memory always. He looked in my direction and winked."

Just then John yelled out, "I got one! I got me a big one! He's a fighter." John pulled back on the pole just enough to keep him hooked, then released a bit, pulled back, released, pulled back and worked the fish until he was able to reel it in. "Looky here. He's a bute! Must be a stone!"

"Hold up, John," said Thomas, "I doubt he'll be weighing fourteen pounds; maybe ten.

Just as Michael began to walk toward John to see if he needed help, he too felt a sudden tug on his line. "Hey, I've got one too!" Michael reeled his fish in and took it off the hook when John yelled out again.

"Wouldn't you know that would happen."

"What?"

"The slippery bugger got away. My ten pounder wiggled right out of my hands. I guess it's true what they say. The good Lord giveth...and the good Lord taketh away.

We all cracked up laughing at the sign of John just staring at the water in disgust as he picked up another worm. I was getting a nibble now as well. I coaxed it toward shore and pulled the line up out of the water. It was the biggest fish I had ever caught and the men were dumbfounded because I wasn't using a worm. The pole I grabbed had a six-hooked, split-tail rebel attached to it and I knew how to work it, since it was my favorite lure back home.

We were having such a good time together that it didn't matter who was doing the catching and who was doing the watching. Shon was using two hooks about three feet apart, with worms and managed to catch two fish at once; another feat I had not witnessed until now. We were going to have a great feast tonight.

Thomas laughed at the sight of the two fish, scratched his chin in disbelief, then said, "Well, Shon, looks like you've got yourself a set of twins. You do know what that means, I'm sure."

Realizing what Thomas was getting at Shon gasped. "Twins!" And then, holding up his fish, he turned and fainted.

CHAPTER 35

Let's Celebrate

"The sun is starting to go down," said Michael. "We better head back before the women, present company excepted, have our heads."

"It's true," added John. "My Sheelah will be filleting me instead of these here fish if we don't get home soon."

We got up from our prospective fishing spots along the river's edge. We heard someone yell out for help.

We looked back and Thomas had slipped into the river and was being rushed towards the falls. The river was high from all the rain they had had recently and it was moving pretty fast. Thomas, although strong minded, was too old and weak to fight the current and kept going under. It was frightening to watch.

Shon was the closet to where he fell in and jumped in himself. "I'm coming, Thomas! I'm coming!"

My head was reeling as I remembered the day I lost my brother to raging waters, and now, here he was in them again, with Thomas!

The other men ran along the bank, towards the falls, hoping to be able to grab them on the way by. Shon swam with the current and reached Thomas pretty quickly. "I've got you," he yelled as he grabbed Thomas by his jacket!

Shon had Thomas, but they were still rushing down that river. The other men were all on the embankment when Michael decided to climb a tree further down and crawled out over the raging river as far as the branch would allow.

Michael wrapped his legs tightly around the branch and leaned over as far as he could. Shon noticed him and stretched an arm upwards, hoping to connect as they sped past. Michael had two hands free and grabbed Shon's wrist with the strength of a clamp. Shon never let go of Thomas and Michael never let go of Shon.

Suddenly the limb broke from the strain of the extra weight and the pull of the river, but it did not disconnect completely from the tree. John was able to climb up on the tree as it lowered into the river and hold on with his free arm as Michael reached over and grabbed Thomas. Once John got all the way up, out of the water, he was able to help Michael pull Thomas in. I prayed the whole time for the good Lord to save my family, and He once again answered, 'Yes'.

When they all got back on shore, we all checked them for injuries. Surprisingly there were only a few bruises and scratches. Everyone was alright and Thomas was laughing.

"What's so funny," asked Shon, exacerbated?! "You almost got killed!"

"No I didn't," said Thomas calmly. "If the good Lord wanted to take me he would have. But I'll tell you one thing, that's the most excitement I've had in a long while!"

We all just looked at the silly old man and lost it. It was just such a crazy sight, seeing him sitting there soaking wet, nearly drowned and having a great time doing it! "We'd better get home and get dried off before we catch our death," said John; "or not only will the women fillet us, they'll gut and fry us too!"

"By the way," said Thomas, "maybe we should keep this one to ourselves. We wouldn't want to be worrying anyone. Shon and I just took a little dip is all."

When we got back to John and Sheelah's, we snuck in the back door and up the stairs. We didn't want to be caught coming in all wet if we could help it, even though we had our cover story in place. "Hey," yelled Sheelah up after us! "What are you hooligans up to, coming in the back door like that and running on the stairs?"

"Nothing dear," John called back. "We just don't want to be smelling like fish when we kiss our darlings is all. The fish is out back on the barrel." He was careful with his tone, but he was no match for Sheelah.

She looked at Maggie and said, "strange men we got there and since when do they care what they smell like for us? I can see Sharon caring, she's a woman. You better believe they're up to no good." Maggie just nodded in agreement.

We all eventually made our way back downstairs and Thomas told them about the fish. "This one here," he held up for his story, "I had to dive in the river to catch. It put up a real battle it did." And then, over his shoulder, "isn't that right fellas?" He was including me in that group as he smiled in my direction.

"Yup, that's right," said John. "Just as he says."

"That it did! A big fight," I said.

"I never saw the likes," said Michael.

And it went on. There was no use upsetting the women with the truth, so we stuck to our 'fish story' and had some extra fun with it.

"Why don't you guys go set up the buffet table," suggested Maggie. "We women can handle the food. Now off with you."

Now it was the girls' turn to get ready for the party. I was already dressed, so I helped the others. We were all in our prettiest party dresses and had put our hair up, adorned with fresh flowers from the garden. It was a special celebration indeed.

The other friends and relatives that were invited came in groups and before long the house was hopping with music and song and dancing. Lots of dancing. Kathie and I drank our ginger ale with fresh ginger root and cranberry juice splashed into it while everyone else enjoyed the fruits from John's barrel. It was a good thing that most of them owned horses or just plain walked to the party, because driving was out of the question after all that ale.

The party went on well into the night with stories of old and new. The news of babies coming into the family and the recent blessing of finding Shon alive. The family of course, as most close families are, was very accepting of Maggie and Thomas' news about Sharon and Shon's tie to them. They were more happy to have us in the family, than worried about any scandal at this point.

I invited all the Irish family and friends back to the Vineyard for a visit as we promised to return to this amazing Emerald Isle again next year.

A few of the people at the party were talking about the festival in Tralee and suggested that I enter the contest for the 'Rose of Tralee'. I thought since I was pregnant that I couldn't enter, let alone win, but was told by Michael that I wasn't showing yet and by Sheelah, that it didn't matter here.

So, after much coaxing, I decided that, just for the fun of it, I would enter the contest, as silly as it may be at my age. The festival began in three days and anyone could show up and enter the contest. 'Rose of Tralee' here I come, after all, my middle name is Rose; I'm half-way there.

CHAPTER 36

The Rose of Tralee Festival

I was told I was very beautiful by my mother, but thought mothers have to say that about their little girls. It was only when the committee, sorting through the many girls trying to enter, accepted me right away, that I thought I may not make too much a fool of myself. The only requirement to enter is that you be of Irish decent. Check. Women from all over the world were allowed to compete in this celebration and I was proud to represent my family.

There were so many people at the festival and I had no idea it was such a big deal. It made me very nervous and I wanted to back out.

"Honey," said Michael, "you're going to do just fine. It's just for fun, anyway; no need to put any undue pressure on yourself, even though I know you can win this."

Practically the whole town of Bantry I was told had come to cheer me on and I didn't want to let them down. "Come on, Sharon, let's go get some of that delicious food I smell," said Michael, trying to distract me.

"Okay. I'm starved, and you're right. I'll be fine."

Meanwhile Maggie and Thomas set off to see the quilts and watch the canning competition. Shon and Kathie went with John and Sheelah to watch the hurling finals.

The announcement came, "Ladies and Gents, Lads and Lassies, over here on the stage we got beautiful ladies for you. Come on over and see who you like for the 'Rose of Tralee!'"

First there would be the talent contest, which I knew nothing about, then we would answer a random question, chosen by the M.C. I chose to sing for my talent, because I loved to sing, and had always sung the Irish songs with my Mom.

So, I began, *"Oh, Danny Boy, the pipes the pipes are calling..."* I knew this song like the back of my hand. Dad sang it constantly when we were growing up. It wasn't just a funeral song in my home, it was a lullaby. When I finished, the crowd actually went wild and I saw many a tear.

"No one can deliver a song like you," said Thomas from the front of the stage. It made me feel like a little girl, singing for my grampa and I felt a release of pressure off of me.

It was time for the announcement of the finalists. The M.C. began, "Ona Dailey, Erin Burke and .... Sharon Brennan." People were yelling out the names of their choices and my family was not to be overdone.

"Go, Sharon!" "Yeah!" .... And one special call came from Maggie's voice. I saw her in the crowd, poking her head around the others, raising her index finger towards me, and simply saying, with confidence and love, "You can do it!" That's all I need to hear. Maggie was my stronghold in this life, other than God, and if Maggie thought I could do it, who was I to question it. I was determined to win this, for her.

The question was asked of Ona Dailey, "Ona, why do you want to be the 'Rose of Tralee'?"

Ona answered sweetly, "Because I always wanted to be a beauty queen and my mom says I'm the prettiest one."

"Thank you, Ona," said the M.C. while the audience clapped politely for her. "Now, Erin, if you will, darling, please answer me this. What makes you the best candidate to represent the 'Tralee Festival'?"

"Well," came Erin's very definite reply, "My grandmother won it thirty years ago and she says it's in our genes. But, I say I am the best candidate to represent the festival because I know a lot about the town's history and can tell others about it."

"Thank you, Erin, that was very nice." More clapping. "And last, but not least, our beauty who came all the way from an Island in the United States, Sharon Rose Walsh Brennan." Everyone who came with me made their presence known and I even heard a whistle from the crowd.

"Sharon," the man began, "Why do you want to represent Tralee?"

"Well, Mr. McCarthy," I began, "you see, I come from another country and I came to visit my family here. I've only been here for two weeks now and I have been made to feel very welcome. I am proud to represent my family and would be even more proud to represent such a beautiful town as your Tralee. Ireland is one of the most beautiful countries I've ever seen and it will be difficult for me to leave here next week. Whether I win or not, I will take this place and all I have met, home with me, in my heart. Thank you for this opportunity."

Now the crowd was really making noise. I guess I said something right. "Well," said Mr. McCarthy, "it seems clear to me," he said to the crowd, "that you want for your 'Rose', Sharon Brennan! Congratulations, Sharon. We are proud to crown you, 'The Rose of Tralee'." And with that, he placed a crown on my head and a little girl gave me a single pink rose.

I was so happy and extremely surprised since so many of the other contestants were beautiful beyond compare and talented. Michael jumped up on the stage and hugged me, and some other family members made their way up as well. I was swept away to ride on the float after being crowned and sashed, holding my one perfect pink rose. I rode on the float in the parade that day that went down the streets of Tralee for all to see and I waived at the people in the streets. There were people hanging out their windows as we passed by and they were dropping confetti down as I reached them. It was an awesome day!

CHAPTER 37

Yachting With Friends

The next morning at the breakfast table, after John had eaten the last sausage on his plate, he sat back, placed his hands on the table and said, "Well, the weatherman says it will be a fine day today and warmer than the usual, and I was talking to my friend Rob, over in Kinsale. He's been kind enough to invite us all for a ride on his boat. Would you be liking that?" As he sipped his coffee, he could see the reaction on our faces. It was a no brainer.

Thomas spoke right up, "I know I would enjoy going out on the water today, John. At home I was in my boat nearly every day and I've been missing it."

John laughed, "Well, Thomas, this boat is a wee bit different than your whaler in America, don't you know. I think you'll all really enjoy this one." He didn't say any more about it since he wanted it to be a surprise. Sheelah winked at him and smiled, knowingly.

Maggie said, "That's really nice of your friend to invite us all. It will be fun and perhaps after we can get a bite at the restaurant over there. What was its name now?" She was trying to remember the name of the place because it had been so long since she had been there, so Sheelah tried to tell her, but Maggie stopped her. "No, no, now...it will come to me. Ah, yes, 'The Vintage Restaurant'. We used to go there as wee girls for special occasions, but I always felt so grown up there. Remember, Sheelah?"

Sheelah went on to describe the birthdays and first communion dinners they had there. She remembered every detail.

Then Maggie asked her, "Is it still there, Sheelah, dear?"

"Aye, that it is," answered Sheelah. "It is still there and the food is just as delicious as it was those many years ago." So it was agreed that the day would be spent in Kinsale, a very impressive town indeed, with its yachting, gourmet restaurants, sea angling, the Cloffs of the Old Head and, of course, it was the time of year for the art show.

We drove into Kinsale and, just when I thought Ireland couldn't get more beautiful, this place was stunning, with its narrow streets along the sea coast. John drove down to the harbor where many regal sailboats lined up along the docks. John and Sheelah's friends, Rob and his wife Mary Kate were walking to meet us. It was the type of day when the sunshine, glistening like diamonds, and the sky, with its combination of Prussian and Cobalt blues, reflected deeply in the water below. It was the kind of place where you could just stand there in awe of God's incredible work. If you have a doubt that He exists, come to this place and you will know that there truly is a God in heaven and he loves us.

Sheelah and John introduced us to Rob and Mary Kate as we all met up on the wharf. The yachts, as well as the sailboats were bobbing in the harbor to the rhythm of the sea.

The moment finally arrived when all of us would get to see this great boat John had been talking about. It was magnificent, donning brass and mahogany which was polished so well it gleamed in the sunshine. On the back of the ship was a brass name plate with but one word on it, 'Baby'. Baby! This was no baby! As we boarded this massive ship, a man dressed in a white uniform stood on the side of the ramp at attention, as if we were royalty.

Walking on, Maggie chuckled and gave John the elbow, "I'd say, John, that you've moved up in the world to be having friends like these."

After we were all on board, I looked back at the harbor as we pulled out, leaned against the railing and just breathed in the salty air, thankful for the peace I now had.

John explained, "Rob is in the Irish export business; and we met long ago when he was just starting out; he's come a long way, he has. Haven't you, Rob, my friend?"

Rob smiled a warm, humble smile and answered, "John is much too modest. I couldn't have done it without him, let me tell you. And I'm ever so thankful to him. Everyone take a seat, have a drink and relax while I tell you the tale of how this all began."

"I was in a pub one evening," began Rob, "having a pint or two, don't you know, and I was talking to the barkeep about starting an export business. I told him it was a good sound idea, but had no mind of how to begin. You know how you get grand ideas sometimes when you're enjoying a pint or two, or three," he joked?"

"Well, this nice fella, sitting beside me, was having a pint as well when he out and said, 'Excuse me, sir, my name is John'. And I said, 'it's nice to meet you, John.'"

"Then he went on to say, 'I heard you talking to the barkeep about an export business and I know I can help you if you'd like.' I say to John, 'John, my name is Rob and I take kindly to any help you're willing to give, but how might you be helping me?'"

"'I know people, Rob,' he says to me, 'people that need jobs, people that can help you here in this country as well as America.' Well, now I really began to listen to this slightly inebriated man, sitting next to me at the bar. He sounded pretty smart. So I said, 'go on, I'm listening.'"

"'To begin with, Rob, a lot of our countrymen travel to America. They can peddle your goods for you. Of course, you'll need a bit of capital to pay them for their work. The people here can help you get the goods to ship and pack them up for delivery.' So, before you know it, here I am; a big time exporter, and John won't allow me to give him anything for his help, so, when he wants a ride on my 'Baby', it's the least I can do."

"I'll bet the fishing is real good around here, John," exclaimed Thomas.

Good Lord, I thought, after our last fishing adventure, and that was on the shore, what could happen on a ship. No, Thomas, no!

John had done some pretty fair angling himself over the years and said, "Best in all the world, Thomas. People come here from all over the world to fish these waters."

Mary Kate politely interrupted their fishing stories. "Would you please follow me to the table? I think lunch is about ready. I see cook rushing about over there."

We walked down a few steps, into an air conditioned dining area. Now that's class. Air conditioning, in a formal dining room, on a boat. There was a large Captain's table set with white linen, crystal glassware and sterling silver settings. Fresh flowers were placed in the center of the table. Glasses were filled with lemon water along with two other wine glasses, soon to be filled with imports from France and Italy. It seemed Rob wasn't just into exporting.

I sat at my place, in between Shon and Michael and admired the dishes. They were unmistakably made of fine china with a pattern I recognized. It was my favorite pattern yet I couldn't afford to buy a set of them. I actually owned a single tea cup and a single saucer. The pattern is Marchesa's Sapphire Plume Collection by Lenox. It seems funny to me that I should be in Ireland, eating off of American dinner plates, which probably cost Rob and Mary Kate way more to import than I would have had to pay right in America.

Michael leaned over and whispered in my ear, "You look so beautiful today, my darling. I love you very, very much."

I gave him a soft kiss and said, "I love you too, Michael. This place is just dripping in romance, isn't it? I'm so happy." This trip had brought us even closer together, especially with the news of the baby.

Then he put his arm around me and said something else. "I have a little surprise for you later; I really think you'll like it."

I really had no patience for waiting, once someone tells me I have to wait. "A surprise, Michael? Oh please tell me now. What is it? It's all I'll think about until you do. Come on, Michael, please?"

He picked up a shrimp from the crystal bowl we were just served, dipped it into the cocktail sauce and placed it in my mouth, ever so slowly. "If I told you what is was, darling, it wouldn't be a surprise, now would it?" He gave me a quick kiss and smiled.

"You're a brat, Michael. It's so not fair." I thought I would pout for awhile.

Everyone was so relaxed as the boat slid gracefully through the ocean's surface. We were far from shore now. There was no land in sight, but I didn't care. The wait staff continued to bring course after course, which included, fin n haddie, coleslaw and au gratin potatoes. For dessert, we were served a scrumptious red velvet cake with a chocolate lining inside, a layer of cheesecake on top and raspberry jam between the two, draped in luscious chocolate ganache.

When we were done eating all of that we were served the traditional, Irish Cream and Mist in different colored tiny crystal cordial glasses. They were nice enough to bring me and

Kathie three glasses, like everyone else, except ours were filled with mango, coconut and pineapple infused milks, one of each. It was exotic and like nothing I had ever had before. A perfect ending to a perfect luncheon.

Some went on the upper deck to play shuffleboard, or fish while others just took a stroll around the ship, out of curiosity. I was told there were five bedrooms on board and a fully stocked bar. Kathie and I opted to sit in the air conditioning a while longer and sip on some iced tea.

We sat with our feet up on foot stools that the staff offered us; I could get used to being spoiled like this. "Kathie, I'm so happy that our babies will be coming around the same time and they can grow up together. I had lost that hope years ago when I lost Shon. But now, my heart is full and it could burst at any moment. It's almost as if one person doesn't deserve to have all this happiness. Life hasn't been kind to me in the past and it's a bit difficult to accept it completely, even now, but I'm trying."

Kathie caught me crying. "Sharon, you don't realize what this has done for Shon. He used to be lost in his work. He never would have taken time away from it to even partake of a small vacation, let alone set out for Ireland. It was as if he was carrying a heavy burden that would knock him down if he didn't stay on the move. So, he just kept moving. I've never seen him so happy. I was an only child and now I have a sister and a whole family. You are like a sister to me, Sharon. I wanted you to know that." When she leaned in for a hug, the boat suddenly stopped with a thud! We're in the middle of the ocean! How can this happen?

Shon and Michael came running to us to make sure we weren't hurt.

"What's going on," I asked in utter fear?

"I don't know," came Michael's earnest answer. "The captain is sending one of his men into the water to see if we hit something. He believes it may be a very large rock or underwater mountain protruding up, possibly a sandbar."

The deck hand was diving into the water when we got topside. When he resurfaced, he reported to the Captain, "I'm afraid we've run aground. We've landed on a sandbar and can't get unstuck without the assistance of another vessel. We're on there good. And one more thing, Captain," he added, reluctantly, "there's a large rock protruding from the sand and we've got it lodged in the hull. I'm afraid we're taking on water, sir."

I was frightened by this news, but Michael and Shon were trying to comfort us and keep everyone calm. "I'm sure everything will be fine," said Shon. "The Captain can radio for help." And then to the Captain, "Isn't that right, Captain?"

"Yes, of course. Now don't you be worrying yourselves. Just stay on deck and rest awhile and I'll be taking care of everything. You may want to get your things together while you're waiting, since we'll most likely be boarding another ship at some point."

Rob chimed in and in his humorous way said, "What's the big deal? We're on a sandbar. How deep can it be?" He was trying to make light of a very scary situation. "But, just the same, we're going to get the life jackets up here in case we need them and prep the life boat. There's really nothing to worry about, folks."

We were relieved, but not completely convinced as we packed up our things and brought them to the designated area. Relieved, a bit, yes...convinced, no. After all, I had seen the movie 'Titanic'.

About half an hour passed and the boat was increasingly taking on water. The Captain appeared with the update. "I'm afraid the radio is down. I've been working on it, but it's jammed. Not to worry, though, we are going to take the life boat out. I'm sure we can make it to one of the nearby islands from here. Now everyone take only what you need and follow me."

Now I was really worried. What would we do when or even if we could reach one of these islands he was talking about? We still have no radio, and my confidence in him knowing these waters is waning since he didn't know there was a large rock in our path before we hit it.

We had to leave the stately ship behind in exchange for what now seemed to be a very tiny boat compared to the waves we were facing. I was terrified of the jagged rocks and waves we may run into as we neared an island in the middle of the ocean. Nevertheless, one by one, we all boarded the vessel as I wondered if we would survive.

CHAPTER 38

A Perilous Journey

The yacht was already going under as we pulled away. The further we got, the more we watched behind helplessly, as hope faded away in the distance. There were thirteen passengers in all including the Captain and crew.

The Irish are very superstitious, so I was very surprised they would allow thirteen on a boat. We had very few supplies packed on board because there wasn't enough room.

The Captain watched the skies and the current for his direction and he believed we were heading towards the Aran Islands. He assured us that once there, he could get help and we would be home sometime tomorrow night. I was really scared about spending the night on this life boat. Sharks, considering my recent encounter with one, were weighing heavy on my mind.

Everyone got as comfortable as possible for our long journey. The plan was for the Captain and his crew to take turns staying up to guide the boat. The other men insisted on taking a watch. That way they could have two awake at once and there would be no mistakes. We started singing Irish songs as a distraction, but we were all frightened, cold and hungry.

We had been in the lifeboat for six hours before I finally gave in to sleep.

The little bit of bread, sausage, cheese and water that we managed to stow was now gone and the situation was becoming desperate as night turned into day. Since Kathie and I were pregnant, we were used to emptying our bladders frequently. How would we manage this on a small boat filled with people?

I told Michael of my problem and he came up with a plan. He was good like that. He took the empty basket that held the food and lined it with the plastic that kept it fresh. He and Shon held up a blanket and I saw no other choice. First me, then Kathie, then the other women. The men would have to do what they did best, over the side. Everyone sang to make it a little less embarrassing. The basket was dumped overboard after each person's turn, then rinsed and put aside for next time.

Even though we were out of water, with light, came hope. The ships cook stood up suddenly, causing us to almost tip over as he yelled out. "Land!"

CHAPTER 39

Island Paradise

It was rough, to say the least, navigating to the shore as we had come upon a very treacherous side of the Island. There were rocks everywhere and a very small beach promised to be our target. Thanks to the Captain's expertise, we made it safely ashore.

Michael and Shon hopped out first to help the others, then pulled the boat onto the shore. We were all so tired and hungry and we just lay on the beach to stretch out and get our land legs back. The earth seemed to still be moving under us.

"Where are we, Captain Jim," asked John? The Captain of our vessel, we just learned, was James Henry O'Shannahan, originally from Dublin.

Jim stood up and looked around. The Island was constructed of cliffs and rocks, pointing straight up to the sky. Surely it had to be uninhabited! There could be no life here, except of course birds. After a moment, he said, "I'm not sure, kids."

With that reply came silence.

Jim went to climb some rocks behind us to see if he could get a better view. Shon and Michael went with him. It looked difficult, but once at the top they would be able to see for miles.

When they returned they reported what they had seen. "There's nothing in sight across the waters," said Jim. "But there is fresh drinking water on the other side of these here cliffs. There is a waterfall and mossy slopes. There seems to be more life over there."

Then Michael said, "It's dangerous for you, Sharon, and you Kathie, in your condition, but we may need to stay over there for awhile. The whole island is surrounded by rough water and jagged rocks, so we can't take the boat around it, we'll have to leave it here. Do you think you two could try to climb?"

"We're strong women, we are," said Maggie, determined enough for all of us. "Of course we can make it!" I could see her concern for Kathie and I as she said this. I also knew she would never leave us behind.

Sheelah looked at Maggie like she was crazy, but knew she had to muster everything she had to climb those rocks, even though she had a terrible fear of heights, which she revealed to us as the men began their ascent. "Well, let's be off then."

Michael and Shon each took a blanket and wrapped what little they salvaged from the lifeboat up in them, using the rope from the boat to tie the packages around their waists. We didn't know what we would need once over there, so they even took the basket to use as kindling.

We set off up what seemed to me a mountain, one footing at a time. We carefully made sure one foot was secure before we moved another one and the guys helped us along the way. Sheelah never looked down or up, only directly in front of her.

It took about a half an hour to get us all safely to the top. The view was one of the most incredible things I had ever seen. Sheelah still could not look. When I saw the waterfall spilling into a clear blue pond and all the lush green moss surrounding the rocks, I felt as if we had stumbled upon an oasis in the middle of a desert. Surely we could stay here until help arrived. But would it?

Continuing the journey, down the other side, we made our way to the bottom of the falls where we drank our fill of fresh water. Sheelah found fresh berries nearby and picked and ate several of them before gathering enough for all.

We were so thankful for them. John and Thomas set off to see if they could scrounge up any other edibles. They weren't gone long when they showed up with apples and truffles of all things. Growing up the way they did, they knew how to find them. They took a chance and struck gold. There were edible mushrooms near the truffle area as well. Thomas was expert on the safeties of mushrooms growing in the wild, so I wasn't worried about eating them.

Shon came up with a way to fashion a hook from a chipped piece of rock and attached it to a single strand he peeled off of the rope. He added a piece of mushroom to the hook and dropped it into the pond. I wouldn't have believed it if I hadn't seen it with my own eyes, but he actually caught a fish, then another and another. There was enough for all to share.

Mary Kate started a fire with some dead wood that was strewn around, twigs and pieces of the basket we had used as a toilet. After great effort, she managed to produce a spark from cracking two rocks together. Rob used a wet stick as a skewer for the fish and laid it across some rocks in the fire. We ate the truffles, mushrooms and fruit raw while we waited for the fish to cook.

It started to get dark and there was a chill in the air. We huddled around our small fire to keep warm. There were no planes or boats in sight and I was losing hope. It began to rain. It was a torrential downpour and almost unbearable with the cold. The rain put out the fire, but Captain Jim had been exploring and found shelter. We ran for it.

There was a cave behind the waterfall and it was very loud inside as the water rushed past, but we didn't care because we were in a dry, safe place for the night.

The men gave the women the two blankets to share and we took full advantage. We all stayed close together in order to find warmth. Shon and Michael went back out of the cave to bring back some wood.

It would be wet, but it was worth a try. Mary Kate found some animal dung in the cave and used it as fuel to start a fire as she knocked some rocks together again. It worked. We then added anything we could find in the cave that was dry before we attempted to add the damp wood from outside. Before long we had a pretty good fire going.

The men took shifts staying awake again in order to keep the fire going and to watch for animals, since there was dung found in the cave, there was a pretty good chance that animal would return.

Morning came, but not without incident. Kathie was very ill. She was shivering uncontrollably and Michael was watching over her. By the way she was breathing and coughing, he surmised that she had pneumonia, which could be fatal to her unborn child.

She was burning up with fever and needed a hospital right away. All we could do was pray and wait. We kept her as warm as possible and Shon was beside himself with worry. Captain Jim took him outside to get more wood and food so that he would stop upsetting Kathie with his worrying.

Kathie wouldn't eat or drink and started talking nonsense.

"She's having hallucinations," said Michael. "She doesn't know what she's talking about or where she is right now. We must get food and water into her! She's completely dehydrated. The baby will not survive if we are unsuccessful."

It had been three days since we left the ship. Kathie's fever had not broken and Michael picked her up and put her into the ice cold water beneath the falls. He had to get her fever down.

"What are you doing," shouted Shon?! "Are you crazy?"

"I know what I'm doing," said Michael. "I must get her fever down or we'll lose her. Now help me!"

Shon did as he was told. He trusted Michael. "Now hold her. She's going to want to struggle when she comes to. She must stay in the water until her fever breaks or she and the baby will surely die."

I jumped into the icy water as well and helped hold Kathie. I talked soothingly to her and she suddenly came to, kicking and screaming. "I'm freezing! What's wrong with you people?! I'm freezing! Let go of me!"

"Hold onto her Shon," said Michael. "Don't let her go yet!" Michael kept checking her temperature as we held her down, then she suddenly went quiet and stopped fighting us. "Her fever has broken; she's going to be okay."

"You saved her life, Michael," I said as we headed back to the cave with Kathie.

Shon helped Kathie back to the cave and we all left so he could help her out of her wet clothes. He would wrap her in blankets and we would put her clothes on the warm rocks out in the sunshine to dry.

As we were walking back down to the clearing, Rob was running towards us. "There's a ship in the lagoon! John is there now. Come on!"

Lagoon? When did they find that? We got Kathie and Shon and followed Rob. There was a ship there, and a lagoon, just as he said.

It seems we were on an island that was an annual stop on a cruise ships schedule. They were very surprised to find us here, so far from any mainland.

The cruise ship was named 'Caroline' and it would take us to Kilkee, which was quite a ways away from where we had started, but we didn't care as long as we were rescued. We took Kathie to the hospital first while Captain Jim and his crew went on their way. Mary Kate and Rob were heading in the same direction, so they went with them, apologizing for what had happened. Captain Jim was very sorry as well.

"There's no need to be apologizing," said John, speaking earnestly for all of us. "It was no fault of yours we hit that rock. Could've happened to anyone."

Kathie and baby were fine, just a bit dehydrated, so she received fluids intravenously before we could take her home.

Finally, we all hopped into the rented van that would take us back to Kinsale and the truck we left there. Michael told the group that we wouldn't be joining them back at John and Sheelah's tonight, but that we would be back tomorrow. No one questioned him, which made me very suspicious.

He helped me out of the van and closed the door. We waved goodbye then Michael put his arms around my waist and pulled me in. "Now, my darling, the Doctor has a prescription for you. We are going to have a day to relax together....alone. We've been on the go since we've been here and I want you all to myself." I felt so safe in his arms. "Are you up for it?"

He had a rental car that we took to get some new, clean, dry clothes, then headed for a hotel. As we walked into Stella Maris Hotel, I kissed my wonderful husband and said, "It's so nice to be alone with you, Michael. I've enjoyed our visit with the family, and the Captain and the crew, *and the rest,* I sang through laughter, but I've been craving alone time with you. After all, this is our honeymoon."

CHAPTER 40

Fanning The Flames Of Love

It was early in the afternoon, just after lunch, when Michael and I drove out to the Fortfield Farm Attraction, which is an Irish working farm. We strolled slowly along the farm pathways, enjoying the sunshine and fall breeze and viewing the birds, llamas, deer, wallabies, swans and even the pot bellied pigs.

"It's very strange, Michael, but I can almost relate to that one over there," I laughed as I pointed to the portly pig.

Michael patted my stomach and offered, "I think you are beautiful, darling, and please keep in mind that your condition is only temporary. They have to go around looking like that for their entire lives. Besides, I barely see a bump on you as yet, and even if you grow to be a very large woman one day, I will still love you, every inch of you, the same as I do now."

I laughed as I took my adoring husbands hand in mine and continued walking. I wondered if our baby was happy and if he or she could feel the loving touch of Daddy and Mommy.

After our walk around the farm, which was more like a zoo, we went to the tea room that they offered on premises, and enjoyed a hot cup of tea and scones with clotted cream and strawberry jam. It was so comforting.

"Thank you sweetie, this was so thoughtful of you. Just walking around here and hearing the birds singing has rejuvenated me," I said to my amazing husband.

He smiled as he helped me out of my chair, as a gentleman would and he said, "You're welcome, darling; now let's go back to the hotel and get you a catnap so you'll be fresh for dinner this evening."

We drove back to the hotel and went up to our room to relax. I loved getting out, but I really loved the resting in between. I laid on the bed, Michael put a quilt over me and laid down beside me, holding me in his arms as I drifted off to sleep.

I woke up to the late afternoon sun peeking through a slit in the curtains. I slipped out from under Michael's arm, careful not to wake him and just looked at his sweet, sleeping face for just a moment before heading to the shower.

In the shower, I noticed that I was beginning to show and I lay my hand gently on my baby and said, "I love you already."

I put on makeup, my pearl necklace and earring set and styled my hair. I tiptoed to the closet and selected an ankle length black skirt and a white three quarter sleeved satin blouse, donning a scooped neckline, just low enough to be pretty. I felt radiant. That glow that everyone talks about when you're pregnant, I could actually see it in the mirror and I felt wonderful.

After dabbing 'White Diamonds' on my wrists, neck and bodice, I walked to the bed and sat quietly beside Michael, brushing the hair out of his eyes. "Wake up Hon, time for dinner."

He moaned a bit, rubbed his eyes and looked up at me in a dreamlike state. "Oh, hi," he said. "Is it that time already? I must have slept a long time. You look gorgeous!"

Then he sat up and kissed me as he pulled me gently back down on the pillows.

"Now, Michael, you're going to get me all messed up again. You don't know how long it takes me to look like this. I don't just wake up gorgeous, you know," I joked.

Michael smiled, "Honey, you don't have to do a thing to look beautiful; you're a natural beauty. I love you." Then he tried to lure me towards the pillows again with a passionate kiss.

"Flattery will get you nowhere mister...come on, hit the showers, soldier," I said, tugging him out of bed.

"Boy, you sure would make a great drill sergeant," he said as he trudged to the bathroom. "Ok, I'll go, but I can't promised I'll be as beautiful as you when I emerge." I shook my head...he's so darned cute, I thought.

We went to the Strand Bar for dinner that night. Michael ordered the Sirloin Steak with garlic mashed potatoes and green beans, something he would've ordered in the states. I got the Roast Spring Chicken, encrusted in caramelized rosemary and served with a mango risotto, something I had never heard of before; it was amazing! Both dinners came with butter biscuits and butter.

We also got an Apple Tart with vanilla bean ice cream and a North Pole dessert. The North Pole was homemade ice cream topped with warm jelly, cream and a raspberry sauce. Sweet and wonderful.

After dinner, when we were bursting at the seams, we decided to walk it off. There was a beautiful beach nearby and it was a crisp evening as we drifted into fall season. The moon was full and bright, hanging in the sky, surrounded by about a gazillion stars. I loved the smell of the ocean and could feel little flickering of the salt water kissing my face as we walked along the ocean's edge.

We didn't walk far before we came across a cove in the rocks. Nestled just inside the cove of this sandy beach, were a blanket and a picnic basket. There was also a lantern propped up against the inside of the cove, which was lit and was the reason this caught my eye.

I looked at Michael and he at me with a huge grin on his face. "When did you do all this," I asked?

"Well, I must confess, my darling. I hired the hotel to set this up while you were bathing."

"You were fake sleeping?! And you expect me to sit there on this cold night with you, Mr. Brennan, and what? What do you expect," I teased.

"I'll keep you warm, Mrs. Brennan," he said as he grabbed me and kissed me so hard I could barely breathe. It was wonderful. "Besides," he said as we came up for air, "as you see, I've also had them prepare a fire pit and I just happen to have a lighter with me. We'll be plenty warm. We could stay all night."

Michael led me to the blanket and helped me sit down. Then he went to light the fire. Coming back over to me, he sat next to me on the blanket.

The picnic basket had an extra blanket in it and he wrapped it around me. This basket was huge and I wondered what else could be in there. To my very pleasant surprise, there was a thermos with hot chocolate in it, and as if that wasn't good enough, there was a small container of marshmallow cream that we could add to our warm drink.

He showed me what else was in the basket, that we could enjoy when we got hungry again, as if that was possible; all the fixings for s'mores. This was all part of the seduction plan and he knew what I liked. Hot chocolate and s'mores.

After just being together for awhile, we toasted the marshmallows over the fire and squeezed them between two graham crackers laced with chocolate bars. This was a very messy project indeed, but I didn't care. We'd have fun cleaning it off of each other.

Michael got that look in his eyes, then laughed out loud. "You have marshmallow cream from the hot chocolate all over your lips and the graham cracker crumbs are stuck to it."

Just as I attempted to lick it off, he leaned over and kissed me, gently, tasting my bottom lip only at first, then the rest. He began teasing me with his kisses until they turned into a tempestuous feeling that would make the sea life take notice.

Michael laid me back on the blanket, using the extra one as a pillow to rest my head. The lantern, the glowing fire, and the full moon created a mood that lit the corner of our little world. The sound of the waves crashing on shore was our music and Michael, the conductor of it all.

Books By:

Roberta M. O'Connell

PERSONAL JOURNEY SERIES

The Book of Love

The Book of Peace

The Book of Joy

The Book of Strength

The Book of Fear

The Book of Truth

The Book of Faith

The Book of Healing

HEALTH

I Want To Live!
Reversing Diabetes

POETRY

To My King

Dear Diary, My Life in Rhyme

CHILDREN'S BOOKS
Under the name: Auntie Roberta

The Adventures of April Rose, I
Know My ABC's

The Adventures of April Rose, The
Christmas Present

NOVEL
By: Roberta M. O'Connell
& Mary Bayne Wojdylak

Secrets In The Tides
A Family Saga

Mary Bayne Wojdylak lives in New Hampshire with her husband, Jim of 48 years, where they are enjoying their retirement together. Mary especially loves trips to the ocean.

In her career, she was Assistant General Manager of a radio station in New Hampshire. She is active in her church and has had many ministries over the years, including going into the women's prison as well as leading a city street ministry to the homeless, where her team sang, while offering them food, clothing and prayer.

Mary and Jim keep busy with their four children, six grandchildren and two great-grandchildren. They are the lights of their lives. Mary's faith in God has been unwavering; trusting in Jesus through all things.

Roberta M. O'Connell resides in Massachusetts with her husband of 32 years. She is active in her church, where she has offered her services over the years as Pro-Presenter Operator, Usher, Teacher, Worship Leader and Lead Singer of the band, "God's Garage", which serves as an outreach band, primarily for those overcoming addictions. Her husband, Dave is the drummer of this band.

Roberta is also the Founder and CEO of Princess Publishers.

Roberta and Mary are a mother and daughter team, who didn't purposely set out to write a book. Mary had back surgery in 2003 and, since they lived in different states, and couldn't get together as much as they would have liked, they started writing letters to each other via e-mail.

One day they decided to have some fun with their e-mails and started a story. One of them started by writing a line and sending it to the other to add on to. This was just supposed to be for fun, but it went on for three months and before they knew it, they realized the story was done and they had something.

After putting the e-mails together and turning it into a complete story, they continued to edit it off and on for the next few years, then set it aside, because, re-write after re-write, it just wasn't right.

Several years later, Roberta decided that it needed to be finished. She wanted her mother to see it in print. So, unbeknownst to Mary, she set out on the arduous task of revamping an entire novel. She changed the perspective in which the story would be told, knowing she needed the audience to feel what Sharon was feeling.

After many months, and keeping the secret from Mom, which was not easy since they are so close and speak often, the book you hold in your hands was completed.

Roberta had two copies printed; one for Mom and one for her. It was a surprise gift she would hand to her mother to read before publishing.

Through laughter and tears, they walked through this book with you and hope you feel every emotion they and Sharon felt throughout this journey from Island to Ireland.

Me & Mom

Roberta & husband, Dave

Mary & husband, Jim

The Waves

I love the waves,
They are so blue,
Some are rough
And some are smooth.

The times the waves are rough,
There is a storm so tough.
The times the waves are smooth,
They shine beneath
the glistening moon.

Oh waves so deep and blue,
I've had such fun with you;
But 'tis getting dark and cold,
So off to home I now must go;
As I was told.

By: Mary Bayne ~ Age 10

I used to sit at Wessagusset Beach in Weymouth MA when I was a child and discovered that I enjoyed writing poetry about the ocean that I loved so much....this was one of them...enjoy!

Mom's Irish Bread

3 Cups All Purpose Flour
½ tsp. Baking Powder
2 Tbl White Sugar
1 tsp. Baking Soda
1 Egg
1 Cup Buttermilk
2 Tbl Melted Butter
Dash of Salt
½ Cup Raisins (optional)

1. Preheat oven to 350° and grease round cake pan.
2. In bowl, mix together all dry ingredients.
   (Toss the raisins in flour before adding)
3. Make a well in center and add the wet ingredients.

4. Stir until all ingredients are absorbed. (I use a wooden spoon)
5. Turn the dough onto floured board and knead for just a few quick turns, handling gently. Pat into a circle and press down to make a round loaf.
6. Place in a pan and cut a cross in the center of the top.
7. Brush with buttermilk.
8. Sprinkle a little cinnamon/sugar on top if desired.
9. Bake 40 minutes or until tapping on bread sounds hollow and top is browned.

Secrets in the Tides

A Family Saga

Photo by: Victoria L. Sullivan

Used by permission: V.L.S.